# THE PEOPLE IN PINEAPPLE PLACE

# THE
# PEOPLE IN PINEAPPLE PLACE

# ANNE LINDBERGH

HARCOURT BRACE JOVANOVICH, PUBLISHERS

SAN DIEGO   NEW YORK   LONDON

Title page illustration by Judith Gwyn Brown

LIBRARY OF CONGRESS CATALOGING IN PUBLICATION DATA
Lindbergh, Anne.
The people in Pineapple Place.
SUMMARY: Ten-year-old August Brown
adjusts to his new home in Washington, D.C.,
with the help of the seven children of Pineapple Place,
invisible to every one but him.
[1. Moving, Household—Fiction.
2. Washington (D.C.)—Fiction.
3. Space and time—Fiction]   I. Title.
PZ7.L6572Pe   1982          [Fic]          82-47935

ISBN 0-15-332878-9    (Library: 10 different titles)
ISBN 0-15-332920-3    (Single title, 4 copies)
ISBN 0-15-332980-7    (Replacement single copy)

Printed in the United States of America

*For my son Charles, who discovered Pineapple Place*

# THE PEOPLE IN PINEAPPLE PLACE

The rag-bag lady stopped in front of the house across the street. August, sitting in the window seat, looked up from his diary to watch her.

It must be garbage day. Although he had lived only a short time in Georgetown, August knew the schedule: trash was collected on Tuesday and Friday mornings. The truck jerked and groaned its way up the street between nine and ten in the morning, but the rag-bag lady (August's private name for her) always came by first.

The rag-bag lady had a scarlet coat with a row of jet-black buttons down one side. On her head was a little black hat with a spotted veil that came down over her eyes, and around her neck was a shining fur piece that looked like a weasel biting its own tail. She always wore black gloves and carried half a dozen shopping bags.

August pressed his nose to the windowpane, trying to see what was written on the shopping bags. One said NEIMAN-MARCUS and one LORD & TAYLOR. Another said SUPPORT THE ARTS! The rag-bag lady reached delicately into the trash can of the house across the street, pulled out something brown and lumpy, and popped it into the bag marked LORD & TAYLOR. Then, as if she had known all along that he was watching her, she turned and waved at August.

Feeling his face grow hot with embarrassment, August dropped the curtain, slumped down on the window seat, and stared at his diary. "REASONS WHY I HATE WASHINGTON, D.C." was written in large capital letters across the top of the page marked *April 9, 1982*. Underneath was his list:

1. Nobody asked me if I wanted to move.
2. Nobody asked my opinion about the divorce.
3. Zachary Judge never gave me back my catcher's mitt, and now there's no way I can make him.
4. I hate cities.
5. I don't know anybody here.
6. I don't want to know anybody here.
7. People who are mothers shouldn't be lawyers.
8. Zachary Judge still owes me $4.79.

August's father had given him the diary on the morning of his move from Vermont to Washington, D.C.

"I know you're not feeling very happy just now," he had told August. "Your mother and I aren't feeling happy either, but we're all three going to have to make the most of our new lives. I thought it might help to keep a diary. If you write down your problems, you sometimes see them more clearly."

It had been a long train ride down to Washington. August had brought several books, but reading in trains always made him feel a little dizzy.

"Why don't you write in your diary?" his mother had suggested.

Opening his diary to *March 27,* August had begun by writing, "Dear Diary, my name is August Brown, and I am ten years old. Today I am moving to Washington."

Then he had stopped to read what he had written. "This is stupid!" he had told his mother as he slammed the diary closed. "It's stupid to write about yourself!"

"Then don't," said Mrs. Brown.

"I'll use it for lists," said August.

The fact was, August was not the kind of boy that keeps a diary. He was the kind of boy that makes lists —lists of what he wanted to do and lists of what he had already done, lists of the things he collected, like chicken wishbones, rubber bands, and lost mittens in winter.

August had collected two shoe boxes full of chicken wishbones, but his mother said they had to stay in Vermont, so he gave them to his best friend, Zachary Judge. He had one hundred and forty-one rubber bands, all different, that his mother had let him bring to Washington. And he had thirty-three lost mittens, also all different. He had never told his mother about those because he was afraid she would make him find their rightful owners.

August tore the list of reasons why he hated Washington out of his diary and thumbtacked it to his bedroom door. Then, although he didn't care for sitters, he went to look for Michele.

August's mother had passed her bar exam that winter, and the reason she moved to Washington after the divorce was that she was starting a new job.

"Can't you just work part-time?" August had asked her. "There's nothing stupider than staying at home with a sitter."

"You won't be staying at home once school starts," his mother reminded him.

"School is stupid too," August had said. "I went to look at it and it stinks, and so do the kids who were playing outside. I wish Zachary Judge could move to Washington."

"Well, he can't," said Mrs. Brown. "So you'll have to put up with Michele until you make some new friends."

Michele was a college student. She was studying at Georgetown University, and she lived in August's house on what Mrs. Brown called an Au-Pair basis.

"Which means," August's mother had carefully explained to both August and Michele, "that she has certain privileges as well as certain responsibilities."

One of the reasons August minded his mother becoming a lawyer was the new way she talked, not just using long words like "privileges" and "responsibilities," but rolling them around in seesaw sentences that were too perfect for August to answer.

Michele's privileges were her room, meals, and use of the telephone. "Of which," August's mother often said in lawyer-talk, "she takes advantage to the letter of the law."

Michele's responsibilities were August. When Georgetown University was back in session and Anthony Hyde Elementary School reopened after spring vacation, Michele would be keeping an eye on August only from when he came home at three o'clock to when his mother came home at six. But there were ten more days before school started, and until then Michele stayed with August all day long. The days seemed very, very long to August.

Michele was in the kitchen, talking on the phone. Cupping her hand over the receiver, she said, "What's up, kid?"

"Can I go to the park?"

"Not now," said Michele.

"Why not?"

"August!" Michele pleaded in a loud whisper. "I'm talking on the phone!"

"Oh. Well, when you get through?"

"Can you hold on for a minute?" Michele said into the receiver. "I've got a problem. Hold on just a minute."

She laid the receiver down on the kitchen counter and turned to August with her hands on her hips, the way she did when she wanted August to think she was angry.

"August Brown, don't you know better than to go interrupting grownups when they're on the phone?"

It had not taken August long to learn that Michele was never really angry. She might pretend she was, but underneath she was the most easygoing sitter August had ever known. He was sorry to bother her while she was on the phone, but what can you do with someone who is on the phone *all the time?*

"You're not a grownup, you're only nineteen!" said August. "Please can I go to the park?"

"I said not now," Michele replied. "Now's not a good time."

"Why not?" August protested. "It's nice outside and it's stuffy inside, and I'm bored!"

"Because your mom said you couldn't go out without me, and I'm busy."

"But you're not supposed to be busy!" August wailed. "You're supposed to be sitting me!"

"So?" Michele laughed. "What do you think I'm doing?"

"You're talking on the phone," said August.

"Then let me finish." Michele turned her back to August and picked up the receiver. "Sorry!" she said to her friend at the other end. "Sorry for the interruption. Go on!"

August tugged at the belt of her jeans. "Please, Michele? Please!"

She elbowed him away. "Do you *mind?*"

August wandered around the kitchen, bumping into chairs, shifting things back and forth on the counter, jerking the drawers in and out noisily. Michele paid no attention.

16

One of the drawers was full of odds and ends: corks and the twisty ties that come on bread bags, pencil stubs and candle ends and one of his mother's earrings, some crinkly pieces of used aluminum foil, and two balloons that the man at the shoe store had given him when he bought his new sneakers. August wondered how the drawer had become so cluttered in the short time they had lived in the new house. His mother must be a collector, just like August! She certainly liked to make lists the way he did. There was one taped to the refrigerator door right now. August looked at it unenthusiastically.

FRIDAY, APRIL 9

1. Before you do anything else, please find the brass knob you unscrewed from the fire screen.
2. Put it back and don't touch it again.
3. Clean up your room before you go outside. Put your dirty clothes in the hamper—don't hide them in your bed.
4. Please, please, *please* write a thank-you note to Aunt Mary Beth for the catcher's mitt she sent you for your birthday. You should have done it weeks ago!
5. If you go outside with Michele, remind her to lock the door.

"Ha!" August said out loud. "Outside with Michele? Fat chance!"

He kicked the refrigerator door, but Michele didn't even turn around. She just shifted her weight from one foot to the other and went on talking.

"I think you did the right thing," she told the receiver earnestly. "Really I do!"

August blew up one of the shoe store balloons and tied a knot in it. He started to bat it around the kitchen, laughing when it hit Michele. Michele batted it right back and went on talking.

"Listen," she said into the phone. "Look at it this way: if that's the kind of guy he is, you don't want to see him any more anyway!"

August batted the balloon over the stove where Michele was boiling water for tea. When it hit the burner, it exploded with a loud bang. Michele shrieked and dropped the receiver.

"August Brown!" she shouted. "Will you get out of my hair before you drive me up the wall?"

"That doesn't make sense!" August shouted back.

The noise had scared him too, and he was horrified to feel tears in his eyes. He rushed out of the kitchen, grabbing his jacket from the hook on the door as he went. Slipping through the front door, he could hear Michele's voice, faint but clear: "Sorry for the interruption. Go on!"

August and his mother had moved into a house on N Street, between 34th and 35th. The streets in Georgetown, like those in the rest of Washington, D.C., follow a logical pattern. The ones running from east to west are called by the letters of the alphabet, and the ones that go north and south are numbered. Crisscrossing here and there are avenues named after the states of the union, although only one—Wisconsin Avenue—actually runs through Georgetown. And from time to time, in unexpected places, you find a few streets with what August called country names, like Reservoir Road, Dent Place, and Pomander Walk.

There was a fire station on Dent Place, and August thought he might go take another look at it. As he ran down the block, he mumbled furiously to himself, " 'Get out of my hair before you drive me up the wall!' What kind of silly talk is that?"

Secretly, though, he preferred Michele's slipshod style to his mother's new lawyer-talk. The other day he had overheard his mother tell a neighbor, "Sometimes August irritates me to the point of distraction!"

Well, she and Michele had a big surprise coming. If August felt like going out, he would just *go* out. Nobody minded if he went out alone in Vermont, so why wasn't he allowed to go out alone in Georgetown too? Those children in the school playground didn't have any grownups with them, and some were even younger than August. Why did he have to have Michele trailing after him wherever he went? It was humiliating!

August stopped short. Half a block away, leaning into a huge gray plastic trash can, was the rag-bag lady. Quick as a flash, August slipped into the shelter of a doorway. He forgot about the fire station and became obsessed with a new idea. Who was the elegant lady who scavenged the neighborhood on garbage days? What did she find in the trash cans to fill her shopping bags? What did she do with it? And where did she live? Today August was going to find out.

**2**

The frail spring sunshine was warm on August's back. Whatever else was wrong with Washington, it was nice to be warm in April. Back home it would be mud season: tenacious lumps of gray snow in the shady parts of the yard and mud everywhere else. It would still be too cold to go out in jeans and a jacket, and when you came back inside and peeled off those tiresome layers of winter clothing (scarves, gloves, snow pants, ski socks, boots), everything would be caked with mud.

But in Georgetown there were tulips and daffodils blooming outside the houses. Yellow forsythia blossoms were bursting out like popcorn, and mockingbirds sang from the shadows of the heavy-leaved magnolia trees.

A sad-sweet feeling swelled up in August's chest, and he recognized it as a yearning to play baseball. But who was there to play with in Georgetown? Except for that sour-faced kid who lived on the corner of 34th Street, there didn't seem to be anyone his age in the whole neighborhood.

The rag-bag lady straightened up and smoothed the

front of her coat with a black-gloved hand. One of the shopping bags was fuller. What had she found? When she was half a block ahead, August ran to the trash can and peered in. All he saw was a stinking heap of grapefruit rinds coated with coffee grounds, greasy paper towels, empty beer cans, and—to his horror—disposable diapers. He slammed down the top and sneezed. Then he felt ashamed. Obviously there was nothing to find after the rag-bag lady had been by. He would get ahead of her this time and explore a trash can up the block.

The rag-bag lady crossed the street to look in the big wire basket outside Sugar's Drugstore. August didn't envy her; he knew from experience that it swarmed with yellowjackets that clung to the sticky ice-cream wrappers. He would have liked to stop and see if she got stung, but he didn't want her to notice him, so he ran up to the corner of 35th and O streets and chose the newest-looking trash can to start his own investigations.

The stench under the clean green plastic lid was even worse than down the street. More diapers, more grapefruit rinds, more coffee grounds. A toy truck missing all its wheels. Eggshells. Mail-order catalogues smeared with bacon grease, and empty envelopes torn in half. A tattered black umbrella with potato peels stuck to every fold. A chicken carcass, a broken bottle, and a pair of little girl's blue-flowered underpants with the elastic dangling from one leg. Groaning with disgust, August salvaged the wishbone from the chicken carcass and put it in his pocket.

Suddenly a sharp, high voice behind him called, "Hey, you! What are you doing?"

He jumped around and saw a small girl with pigtails and a runny nose, standing in front of her open front door.

"Aw, nothing!" he said. "Just looking."

"Looking in the *garbage?*" The little girl wiped her nose on the back of a plump, smudged hand (August guessed she had been playing with colored chalk) and giggled.

"Aw, go back inside and blow your nose, why don't you?" August grumbled. "Go find your mother and tell her she needs you!"

"That's our trash can!" squeaked the little girl. "That's *my* garbage, and that thing you put in your pocket is mine too. Give it back or I'll call my mommy!"

Her voice grew alarmingly shrill, and August decided to retreat. Dropping the lid back on the can, he fled around the corner and crouched behind a bush on O Street. He could still see a patch of the rag-bag lady's red coat from where he was hiding. Would she choose the new-looking trash can next? He was anxious to see if she found something he had overlooked.

The rag-bag lady was in no hurry. She rummaged through the basket outside Sugar's, yellowjackets or no yellowjackets. August saw her slip several things into her shopping bags. The little girl around the corner finally stopped calling her mother, and August heard a door slam. Only then did the rag-bag lady cross the street. August peered around the corner. Seven times the rag-bag lady reached into the new green trash can and pulled out things that disappeared into her shopping bags. For the life of him, August couldn't make out what those things were.

More intrigued than ever, August followed the rag-bag lady up 35th Street to Volta Place. There she turned right and worked her way back to 34th Street. At the corner of 34th and Volta she turned right again and moved downhill to P Street, where she turned right for the third time. She seemed to have a definite plan for her work and knew which cans were worthwhile opening and which were not. She often went by three or four without giving them so much as a glance, but when she reached the next, she would lift the lid with confidence. The shopping bags were bulging, and still August could not tell what they contained.

Suddenly August heard a jerky creaking and rumbling noise. The garbage truck was coming! August was glad because, after keeping still in shady places for so long, he was feeling chilly. He hoped the rag-bag lady would hurry now.

But the approaching garbage truck didn't seem to bother her at all. She spent a minute or so inspecting a large packing box filled with trash, then straightened up, gave her shopping bags a little shake, and turned calmly into a narrow alley halfway down the block.

In all his explorations of Georgetown, August had never noticed that alley. It was squeezed in unobtrusively between number 3415 P Street, which was a tall yellow brick house with gray shutters, and number 3413, which was a short pink brick house with white shutters. Nailed to the side of the pink house was a faded street sign that said PINEAPPLE PLACE, N.W.

August let the rag-bag lady get a little way ahead of him before turning into the alley. Good, it was a dead-end street. She couldn't escape from him now!

Pineapple Place didn't begin to look like a real street until August got through the dark, windowless passage between the pink brick house and the yellow brick house. But then the concrete pavement came out of the shadows and abruptly changed to cobblestones. August had a sudden, delightful impression of trees and flowers and sunlight.

Six narrow brick houses, three on each side of the street, were set back behind six patches of ornamental gardens—that is to say, five gardens and one junkyard. The people in the pale-green house, the brick-red house, and the blue house with black shutters on the left side of the street, and the people in the gray house and the blue house with yellow shutters on the right side of the street had all planted trim round bushes and spring flowers, neatly sectioned off by railings. But the people in the last house on the right—the one whose dingy white paint was peeling, the one missing a shutter from the second-story window, the one with a DANGER! sign on the broken front step—obviously thought their garden was the best place to keep last year's Christmas tree (with tinsel tangled in the branches), two rusty tricycles, a broken-pronged rake, a three-wheeled baby buggy, and a tottering tower of flowerpots still filled with dried-up plants.

"I'll bet you anything," August said to himself, "that's where the rag-bag lady lives."

The rag-bag lady, however, had disappeared, and there was no sign of life in any of the houses. August waited in the alley. After going to so much trouble, he wasn't going to walk away defeated. "What goes in must come out!" he told himself firmly.

The sound of the garbage truck faded into the distance. A marmalade cat appeared from behind an azalea bush, stretched in the sunshine, and twisted around to lick the fur behind its left back leg. A delicious, sugary smell wafted out an open window of the pale-green house.

"What a nice place to live!" August thought. "Much nicer than our house on N Street. Almost as nice as Vermont!"

He killed time by trying to decide which house he would live in if he had his choice. Perhaps the pale-green one—it was the most cheerful.

"What I like about this place," August said to himself, "is it's so quiet. Almost country quiet!"

At that moment a loud shriek came from the shabby white house with the junkyard garden. The front door burst open, and a ginger-haired girl came stumbling down the steps, followed by a red-headed boy about August's age. The boy was shouting and the girl was shrieking, and they ended in a squirming heap on the sidewalk. Two older girls, so alike that August knew they must be twins, ran out and tried to pull the children apart, scolding angrily, while a very small girl with bright-red curls stood in the doorway with her eyes squeezed shut and her fingers in her ears, screaming, "Mummydaddymummydaddymummydaddy!"

August burst out laughing, but stopped abruptly when a soft voice behind him said, "They're always like that, you know. Some days you can't hear yourself think!"

A girl August's age was standing in the doorway of the pale-green house. She had mouse-colored hair tied into ponytails with two ribbons that matched her hazel eyes. She was neatly dressed in a fresh white blouse, a green plaid skirt, and well-polished lace-up shoes. But her knee socks and her cardigan had been knitted in wild, streaky patterns with more colors, August guessed, than there were in his fifty-piece pen set. He had never seen anything like it, and he tried politely not to stare.

"My name is April," said the girl, "April Anderson."

"That's funny!" said August. "My name is August. Isn't it a coincidence that we should meet each other?"

"Oh, no!" the girl said gravely. "It's not a coincidence at all."

August was wondering if April knew what "coincidence" meant, when out of the gray house across the street came the rag-bag lady.

"I brought you the friend you asked for!" she called

to April. "Will he do? He was the best I could find at short notice."

"He'll do fine!" April answered. "Thank you very much!"

"What do you mean I'll do fine?" August asked. "She didn't bring me here—I was tracking her."

"And a very nice job you made of it, too," said the rag-bag lady, nodding approvingly. "I hope it didn't seem too long, but I'm not master of my time. Tuesday and Friday mornings or not at all, and then where would we all be?"

She waved to April, ran back into her house, and shut the door.

August's jaw dropped with astonishment.

"There's nothing to be upset about," April reassured him. "She just knew I was lonely, so she found me a friend."

August looked at the noisy, tumbling cluster of children up the street and wondered how anyone could be lonely with such neighbors.

"Oh, them!" said April, following his glance. "They're all right—when they're not fighting with one another. Actually, Mike is my best friend."

"Mike?" August repeated stupidly.

"Michael O'Malley. That's the red-headed boy. The others are his sisters. The twins are named Theresa and Elizabeth. Then there's Michael and next there's Jessica, and Margaret is the baby. But everybody just calls them 'Tessie-Bessie-Jessie-Meggie-and-Mike.' "

"You don't know how lucky you are," said August. "There are no kids at all on my block except one, and he doesn't count. I wouldn't like him even if I knew him."

April nodded wisely. "We have one like that too. He lives over there."

She pointed at the blue house with yellow shutters, across the street. "His name is Jeremiah Jenkins, and he's awful. But I have to put up with him all the same. That's the trouble—we're together day after day, year after year, and I never meet anyone new."

August felt sorry for her, but he didn't know what to say; he had not run up against the problem before.

"Well, never mind!" said April more cheerfully. "You're here now, and that's all that matters. Let's go inside. I'm making fudge!"

August didn't get home until a little past noon. When he turned into N Street he saw Michele on the doorstep, waiting for him. Only when he noticed the expression on her face did he realize how long he had been gone and remember that he ought not to have gone at all. But August was too excited to feel guilty.

"Michele, guess what!" he shouted, breaking into a run. "You'll never guess what!"

The worried look in Michele's eyes hardened into anger. "Where on earth were you?" she demanded. "By the time I got off the phone, you were out of sight. Where did you go?"

"Just up the street," said August. "I'm sorry, Michele, but I can explain. Wait until you hear how—"

"But, August," Michele wailed, "you've been gone three hours! I had to call your mom at her office. She's probably calling the police right now!"

"Oh, gosh, I'm sorry, Michele!" said August, brushing past her into the house. "I forgot. I was having so much fun, and I met this girl and we—"

"Call your mom!" Michele shouted after him. "Call her right now, do you hear?"

"And we made fudge!" August shouted back. "I brought you some."

He dialed his mother's number at work and told the secretary who he was. Hardly a second passed before his mother was on the phone.

"What's up?" she demanded in an ominous voice.

August switched the receiver to the other hand as if it were a hot potato. "I'm back," he said. "I'm sorry, Mom. I just got so mad that I had to run somewhere, and then I followed this crazy lady in the street and I met a girl who—"

"We'll talk about it when I get home," his mother interrupted, "and I don't want you out of Michele's sight until this evening."

"Not even to go to the bathroom?" August protested. But his mother had already hung up the phone.

"What did I tell you?" said Michele. "Now you're in for it! Why did you do it?"

"I was mad," said August. "I'm sorry you were worried, but why can't I go out alone? Nothing's going to happen to me, and all the other kids get to go out alone."

This was a risky statement from a boy who repeatedly complained that there were no other kids at all in the neighborhood, but Michele didn't catch him up on it. Instead, she agreed.

"You're right," she said. "I told your mom it was a safe neighborhood, but maybe she thought I was too lazy to go out with you. Anyway, rules are rules. I just hope she doesn't fire me. I like living here."

"Yeah," said August, shuffling his feet, "as a matter of fact, I don't mind having you here." This was the closest thing to a compliment (which he intended it to be) that August had said in a long time.

"Well," said Michele more cheerfully, "I forgive you, anyway. Look, the mail came while you were gone. There's a package for you."

August reached into his pocket and pulled out a large square of fudge, which he broke into two uneven pieces. He gave the bigger piece to Michele before opening his package.

It was a fairly small package, clumsily wrapped in brown paper that had once been a grocery bag. Inside was August's catcher's mitt and an envelope containing a dollar bill, three dollars and seventy-nine cents in loose change, and a note from Zachary Judge:

Dear Aug,

Greetings. I hope you're doing fine in Washington. I'm doing awful because my dad just got transferred to Chicago. What's there to do in Chicago? Here's your mitt and here's the money I owe you so now we're quits.

Your friend,
Zack

Michele looked over August's shoulder, chewing her

fudge noisily. "Anything interesting?" she asked with her mouth full.

"Just my catcher's mitt. And some money he owed me."

"Who?" And without waiting for him to answer, Michele added, "Hey, that's great! Want to go out and play ball?"

"I don't know," said August glumly. "I guess my mom wouldn't want me to."

"She said not to let you out of my sight," said Michele, grinning, "so if I feel like playing ball in the Hyde School playground, that means you have to come too."

August slouched out of the house and waited while she locked the door. Zachary's letter was a real shock. His own moving away had been bad enough, but now that Zachary was moving too, it was as if the whole state of Vermont had been wiped off the map.

"But my dad still lives there," he reminded himself. "My Dad lives in Vermont, and I can stay all summer with him."

August slapped his baseball rhythmically into the mitt, but it didn't give him the good feeling he had been looking forward to.

Michele gave his shoulder a little shake. "Cheer up!" she advised. "Your mom won't kill you. She'll probably get mad at *me,* if anything."

August shook his head. "It isn't that, it's something else."

"I bet it's just living in a new place," said Miche
"You'll feel better when you start school and get
know some other kids, believe me."

Looking at Anthony Hyde Elementary School, .
gust doubted he would feel much better when he joi
the fourth-grade class. Its grim brick façade was bro
by an undignified red door that was about as convin
as the smile on his doctor's face when she came tov
him with a tetanus booster. Except for a faded p
valentine glued to one of the panes, the windows
dark and dreary. The playground was a bleak exp
of asphalt, and the baby slide and swings set back i
corner looked abandoned and forlorn.

"Hey, there's your friend from down the st
cried Michele.

The sour-faced boy whom August had mentio
April was dribbling a basketball and taking rand
shots at a hoop that no longer had a net.

"He's not my friend," said August.

"Ask him if he wants to play catch," said M
"Go on, ask him! How are you going to get t
anybody if you act so shy?"

August turned his back to the sour-faced l
slowly moved away, slapping the ball into his c
mitt.

"Okay, I'll ask him for you," said Michele

She walked over to the boy and said, "Hi! W
new neighbors. Want to play catch?"

The sour-faced boy stopped looking sour :

33

ment. Then he glanced at August's back and shook his head. "Thanks anyway," he said, "I have to go home for lunch."

"I told you so," August said smugly when the boy had left.

"You told me what? He looks like a nice kid. But you weren't exactly inviting, were you? Well, better luck next time!"

They threw the ball back and forth for a while. Michele was not very good at catching, and she couldn't throw at all. Either she threw underhand, which was like playing ball with a baby, or she heaved the ball any which way in an awkward overhand and August had to crawl into the bushes to retrieve it. But she was having so much fun that he didn't like to hurt her feelings.

"Oops, I'm sorry!" she said when the ball went flying across the street for the fifth time. "I guess I need some practice. It doesn't act like a Frisbee!"

"It's not supposed to," August said scornfully, tossing her an easy one.

Michele chased it all the way to the baby slide. "This will burn up the calories in that fudge, anyway!" she said, panting.

August tried hard to be patient, but his mind began to wander. He wanted to spend the next day in Pineapple Place with April Anderson, but what would it look like if he arrived with Michele in tow? Besides, Pineapple Place was his own discovery, and April was his own

private friend. Wasn't there some way he could convince his mother to let him go alone?

He tried to argue with her that evening, but she was too upset to listen. "Stop trying to change the subject," she told August. "I want you to concentrate on what I'm saying. Don't you think you're old enough to have some consideration for others?"

For the seventh time August replied, "Yes, but—" and sighed as his mother went on without hearing.

"Michele was frantic," Mrs. Brown continued. "I didn't know whether to call the police or leave work and look for you myself. And with this new job, I can't just get up and leave the office for half the day."

August didn't know how many times he had said "I'm sorry" that day, but he said it again.

"You're sorry! It's all very well to say you're sorry, but don't you understand that after you behave like this, I can't really trust you?"

The more August stared into his mother's cross, worried face, the more he wished he could reassure her, but when he tried to think of the right words his mind went blank. "Yes, but—" he said for the eighth time.

By a stroke of luck, there was a knock at the front door. His mother went to open it and came back smiling.

"Can the session be suspended?" she asked. "One of our neighbors called on us, and she'd like to meet you."

August was surprised to see as much relief in his

mother's face as he felt himself. Together they went to the living room and shook hands with a blond woman dressed in jeans, with friendly smile wrinkles at the corners of her eyes.

"How do you do?" August said politely.

"I've been dying to meet you," said the woman. "I have a son just your age. I can tell you're going to be the best of friends!"

"Where do you live?" August asked suspiciously.

"Right down there on the corner," she said, pointing. "You've probably seen Peter in the street. Peter Snyder-Smith. He doesn't have much to do now that school's out, so he just wanders around the neighborhood."

August had a sinking feeling that Peter Snyder-Smith was none other than the sour-faced boy with the basketball, but he was more interested in something else the woman had said.

"Alone?" asked August.

Mrs. Snyder-Smith looked startled. "I beg your pardon?"

"Does he wander around the neighborhood alone? How old is he?"

"He's ten, like you," said Mrs. Snyder-Smith, "and of course he goes alone. I can't spare the time to go with him, and anyway, it's perfectly safe."

"You see!" shouted August. He whirled around and smiled triumphantly at his mother.

"Hold it!" said Mrs. Brown. "Calm down. Let's get the facts straight."

"We're from Vermont," she explained to their guest.

"We're not used to city life. I had the impression that it was unsafe for children to go out alone in cities. I've heard from friends in New York—"

"But this isn't New York City," said Mrs. Snyder-Smith, "it's Georgetown. And this is a very friendly neighborhood. Peter has been playing outside alone since he was seven. He has to be home before dark, of course, but we've never had any problems."

August's mother looked undecided. "Well, if the other parents think it's safe—"

"Oh, it's perfectly safe," said Mrs. Snyder-Smith. "You'll look back and laugh at yourself once you get accustomed to the neighborhood. You'll find you recognize practically everyone you see."

"I've seen some pretty shady-looking individuals," said Mrs. Brown. "Have you by any chance noticed that extraordinary woman who goes through the trash cans? She's quite methodical about it, and she's always so neatly dressed—black gloves and a hat with the silliest little veil!"

Mrs. Snyder-Smith laughed. "My dear, that's the latest fashion: the thirties look! Someday I'll ask her where she buys her clothes."

Mrs. Brown looked doubtful. "She may be a little unbalanced."

"Nonsense. She's perfectly harmless," said Mrs. Snyder-Smith. "Just a wee bit eccentric, that's all."

"I wonder where she lives," said Mrs. Brown.

"Nobody knows," said Mrs. Snyder-Smith. "She's our local mystery."

"I know," said August. "I followed her there this morning. She lives in Pineapple Place."

"Pineapple Place?" Mrs. Snyder-Smith repeated. "What a quaint name! I've never noticed the street. What part of town is it in?"

"It's close to here," August told her, "on P Street, between 34th and 35th."

Mrs. Snyder-Smith shook her head firmly. "I'm afraid you're mistaken," she said. "I walk my dog along P Street every day, and I've never seen it. Are you sure you don't mean Pomander Walk, across from Volta Park?"

"Positive," said August. "I was there this morning. I can see how you'd miss it, though. It doesn't look like much until you get inside."

Mrs. Snyder-Smith smiled condescendingly and patted August's knee. "I've lived in Georgetown for eleven years, my dear boy. I've walked my dog up every alley in the neighborhood, and I can assure you there's no such thing as Pineapple Place."

The next day was Saturday. August's mother liked to sleep late on Saturday mornings, and Michele was off duty. August himself was up and dressed at half-past six, but what is the use of getting up early if you can't get away early? Mrs. Brown had told August that she expected to see him at breakfast, Pineapple Place or no Pineapple Place.

Naturally they ate breakfast together on weekdays too, but August's mother was in such a hurry that she grabbed a cup of coffee and a piece of toast and was too busy chewing to talk. But on Saturday and Sunday mornings they sat at the table and had a real meal and talked. They were having lox and bagels this morning; August could tell by the smell in the refrigerator. He loved lox and bagels, but he wished that for once his mother would come down early and get it over with.

Michele padded downstairs in her bathrobe and slippers, holding a Frisbee. She opened the refrigerator door and poured herself a glass of milk. "Lox and bagels, huh?" she said, sniffing. "Maybe I ought to stay."

"Why, where are you going?"

"I'm playing Frisbee with some friends. We're having a picnic."

"Dressed like that?"

"What do you think!" Michele wiped her milk mustache on her bathrobe sleeve. "Want to come too?"

"Thanks anyway," said August, "but I'm invited to spend the day with my friend April."

"Oh, yeah, Pineapple Place!" Michele laughed as she went upstairs to dress. "Hope you find it!"

August's mother said the same thing at breakfast: "Are you sure you can find this place again?"

"Of course I can!" said August. "It's not that far away, I tell you. Just a couple of blocks from here."

"Mrs. Snyder-Smith seemed so sure it wasn't there," his mother reminded him.

This worried August too, but he was afraid that if he said so she wouldn't let him go. "Maybe I got the name wrong," he admitted, "but I know exactly how to get there. And they're really nice people. You'd like them, I promise."

Even after breakfast was eaten and all the dishes were cleared away, August couldn't get started because his mother insisted on packing him a picnic lunch.

"Mrs. Anderson will feed me," he argued. "She invited me, didn't she?" He hopped from one foot to the other with impatience.

"Given my experience as a parent," said Mrs. Brown, "I ought to know when a picnic lunch is in order."

More lawyer-talk, August thought in disgust. He kept zipping and unzipping his jacket in irritation. "April invited me for lunch," he repeated, "and now I'm going to be late."

"It's only ten-thirty," said Mrs. Brown. "I packed a sandwich for April too, just in case."

Then she winked at August and added, "Don't forget to give my regards to the bag lady!"

August was halfway down the block before it occurred to him that his mother thought he was making the whole thing up. It made him furious. Did she think she was packing a sandwich for an imaginary friend? But why did she believe a total stranger rather than her own son? August would take his mother's word over Mrs. Snyder-Smith's any day of the year.

It was a relief to see April waiting for him at the entrance to Pineapple Place. There she was, as real as August himself, her hazel eyes glowing with excitement. And there on the wall of number 3413 P Street was the sign that said PINEAPPLE PLACE, N.W.

"You're real!" August shouted, running toward April.

Anyone else might have thought this an odd way to say hello, but not April. "Oh, we're real enough," she said. "It's just a question of timing."

August misunderstood. "I know I'm late," he apologized. "I was ready on time, but my mother insisted on packing me a picnic lunch."

"It's a good thing she did," said April. "We all have picnic lunches too."

"We?" August looked behind April and saw six children standing in a row. Five of them he recognized as the O'Malley family. The sixth, a sulky-looking boy with round blue eyes and dark curls that grew almost to his collar, must be Jeremiah Jenkins. All six children wore socks and sweaters knitted with the same streaky multicolored yarn as April's socks and sweater, and each child was holding a paper bag.

"Mr. Sweeny is feeling poorly," April explained, "so he told us to go someplace else for the day. We tend to be on the noisy side, you know."

"Who is Mr. Sweeny?" August asked.

Mike looked scornful. "Don't you know anything? He's the most important person in Pineapple Place, that's all."

"How should August know about Mr. Sweeny?" said April. "He didn't even know about Pineapple Place until yesterday. The point is, Mr. Sweeny is very old and he doesn't like noise."

Jeremiah Jenkins gazed innocently at August through unbelievably long, curly eyelashes. "Some of us," he simpered, "are noisier than others."

From what he knew of the O'Malley children, August suspected this was true, but he agreed with April that Jeremiah was, in her words, perfectly awful. The O'Malley children obviously agreed too, because Jeremiah's remark was answered by a loud chorus of catcalls.

"You see?" said Jeremiah smugly.

"Well, whoever makes the noise, we're all taking it to

the park this morning," April said briskly. "Meggie O'Malley, you button up that sweater. It's not as warm as you think!"

August was learning that April, although not the oldest child in Pineapple Place, was the ringleader. All the others, including Tessie and Bessie, the twelve-year-old twins, listened to her with respect.

Meggie buttoned up her cardigan with clumsy, baby fingers and looked trustingly at April. "Where shall we go? Can we go to Volta Park?"

"Volta!" said April scornfully. "We have all day. We don't need to go to Volta. Let's go to Montrose!"

Volta Park was right in the neighborhood, only a few minutes' walk away. It covered the area of a city block and had a children's playground, a basketball court, several tennis courts, and a public swimming pool that August was looking forward to using come summer. Montrose Park was on the other side of Wisconsin Avenue, almost half an hour's walk away, but it was enormous. In fact, it didn't really stop at all, because if you went far enough it turned into Rock Creek Park, which is the biggest park in Washington, D.C., and goes on for miles and miles.

August had never been to Montrose Park, but his mother had taken him to the Dumbarton Oaks Gardens, which are right next-door. When he and the children from Pineapple Place reached the big iron gates, he stopped and said, "Hey, why don't we have our picnic here?"

"Here?" April looked doubtfully at the high brick

43

walls surrounding the gardens. "What do you mean?"

"It's full of flowers," said August, "and fountains and secret gardens, and there's a bamboo maze. Let's have our picnic here!"

The O'Malley children giggled and nudged one another. April was astonished. "Do you know Mr. Bliss?" she asked.

"Mr. Bliss?" August repeated. "Who's that?"

April tugged at his arm. "This place belongs to Mr. Bliss," she said firmly. "It's private property. We couldn't get in if we tried."

August pointed to a metal plaque on the wall next to the gate. "Open daily, two to five," he read aloud. "I went there just the other day with my mother."

"Who cares where you went with your mother?" said Mike. "When you're with us, you have to do what we do. Who invited you, anyway?"

"*I* invited August," said April. "What's wrong with you, Mike? I thought you'd be glad to have a new friend!"

Mike scowled and turned his back.

The younger children were growing restless. "It's no use standing here arguing," said April. "I guess this place is public after all, but it's nowhere near two o'clock. Let's go."

Nothing August said could convince her otherwise.

The younger children begged to play on the swings in Montrose Park, but instead, April led them down a steep road dividing the park from Dumbarton Oaks. At the bottom of the hill she turned left on a rocky path that led through the woods to a little wooden bridge over a stream. The path wound on along the stream, arriving finally at an open meadow.

April stopped here and looked triumphantly at August. "This is the best place in the whole of Georgetown for a picnic!" she boasted. "And hardly anybody knows about it."

August had not seen such a beautiful spot since he left Vermont. The meadow was knee-high with wild flowers, and a breeze swept patterns through the uncut grass. The only sounds were country sounds—birds and the stirring of high branches, and the bubbling stream. There were no houses anywhere, no streets, no cars. And this morning there was not a soul in sight except for August and the children from Pineapple Place.

Mike O'Malley let out a blood-curdling whoop and galloped into the meadow. "Let's hunt for crawfish!" he shouted.

April's eyes lit up. She bent over to unlace her shoes. "Leave your shoes and socks here," she ordered the others. "We don't want to lose anything this time. And stuff your socks in your shoes so we can tell them apart."

Seven pairs of multicolored socks were stuffed into seven pairs of brown leather lace-up shoes. August's white tennis socks and sneakers looked out of place among them. Next to the pile of shoes and socks were eight plump paper lunch bags.

Anyone who came by and saw those shoes and picnic bags, August told himself, would think, "Somewhere near here eight children are having a very good time!"

Only yesterday morning he had written in his diary that he didn't know anybody and didn't want to know anybody. August smiled at his good luck as he rolled up the legs of his jeans and joined the others.

The stream was icy around his ankles, but it felt delicious. Gripping some low branches to keep from slipping on the mossy rocks, he watched carefully while Mike and April showed him how to catch crawfish.

First they would choose a spot where several rocks were clustered together, looking like a safe place to hide if you were a crawfish. Then one of the children would quickly flip over a rock. Often there was nothing underneath, but sometimes several crawfish would scoot out, looking for a better place to hide. Then came the tricky part: you had to cup your hands around them and pop them into a container filled with water.

"But don't try for the big ones," April warned. "They pinch!"

So the big ones were allowed to escape, and actually most of the little ones escaped as well. It was exciting work at first, but soon the twins complained that their feet were aching from the cold.

"Mrs. Sweeny has enough to keep her busy," they said. "She doesn't want to nurse seven cases of pneumonia!"

They made the younger children run relay races in the meadow to warm up, but April and Mike wanted to stay down by the stream.

"Unless you're bored," April told August politely.

Bored? He hadn't had so much fun in weeks! "Don't be silly," he told her. "And the water isn't really cold. Why, back in Vermont there's still ice on the streams!"

"You don't catch pneumonia from cold water, anyway," said Mike scornfully. "You catch it from germs. Any fool knows that."

August remembered what the twins had said. "Is Mrs. Sweeny a nurse?" he asked.

"More or less," said April. "She wasn't exactly trained to be one, but she picked it up when Mr. Sweeny started feeling poorly. And my father is a doctor, so he taught her a lot. We needed a nurse, you see, for epidemics. Once the whole street got the flu, and once all seven of us children had the measles at the same time. That was eleven years ago, and Mrs. Sweeny wasn't a very good nurse yet, so my father had to do most of the work."

Mike let out a delighted squeal as he turned over a rock and sent half a dozen crawfish skittering in different directions. August darted one way and April another. They managed to capture two of the crawfish, but the others got away.

"I think we have enough now," said April. "I'm starving! Let's have lunch."

There was something odd about what April had just said. August thought it over as he dried his feet and pulled on his socks and sneakers. He ate a hard-boiled egg, still puzzling. He unwrapped a tuna-salad sandwich and took a huge bite of it. Then he nearly choked, because it finally occurred to him what was wrong.

"But, April!" he exclaimed. "You weren't even born eleven years ago. Neither were Mike and Jessie and Meggie and Jeremiah. And the twins were only one year old!"

April blushed, and Mike O'Malley dropped the peanut-butter and jelly sandwich that he had been stuffing into his mouth.

"I *knew* it was a bad idea to let him come!" said Mike. "Why doesn't he mind his own business and let us mind ours? You're going to have to choose between him and me, April!"

As he went stamping off, April shouted after him, "I choose both of you!" But Mike pretended not to hear.

"Never mind him," April told August. "Let's go play hide-and-seek with the others!"

August shook his head. "First I want to know something. None of you were born eleven years ago—except the twins. So how could all seven of you get the measles?"

"It was a slip of the tongue," said April.

She became very busy picking up the shells of August's egg and putting them in his sandwich wrapper. "If there's one thing I can't stand, it's litter," she said priggishly.

"And if there's one thing I can't stand, it's dishonesty," August retorted.

April blushed again and stared at him indignantly.

"I'm sorry," said August. "You don't have to explain anything if you don't want to, but at least you ought to say so. And come to think of it, that's not the only question I'd like to ask you."

"What else?" April asked in a quavering voice.

"Well, like why did you act so funny about Dumbarton Oaks, for instance? Who is Mr. Bliss? And who is the rag-bag lady, for that matter? And how come Mrs. Snyder-Smith says there's no such thing as Pineapple Place?"

April put aside the picnic bags and leaned back in the grass. "What do *you* think?" she asked. "Are we real or aren't we real?"

"Of course you're real," August said impatiently. "What does that have to do with it?"

"Everything," said April, "because as long as you're sure we're real, you won't have any trouble believing the rest of it. And I guess I do owe you an explanation." She sighed. "I thought it would be easy to have a new friend, but I guess nothing is easy when you live the way we do. Mrs. Pettylittle warned me you'd be making trouble."

"Who is Mrs. Pettylittle?" asked August.

"I guess I'd better tell you the whole story," said April, and this is the story she told:

"When it all began, we lived in Baltimore. It was just after my tenth birthday. That was in 1939."

"But you're ten *now,*" August interrupted, "and this is 1982. How can you be ten for forty-three years?"

"If you keep on asking questions," April snapped, "how can I tell you the answers? Be quiet and listen.

"So I was telling you, I was ten in 1939, and Pineapple Place was exactly the same as it is now, except it was in Baltimore. We were just six families: my parents and I, Mr. Theophilus Todd, and the Sweenys on the north side of the street; the O'Malleys, Mrs. Jenkins, and Mrs. Pettylittle on the south side. Of course, we're facing east and west here in Georgetown, but it all comes to the same thing."

"You've been ten for forty-three years," said August dreamily, "and your mother lives with your father, and you've all been together the whole time!"

"If you don't stop interrupting, I won't tell you the story," April told him.

"I'm sorry," said August. "Go on!"

"Well, we were living different lives back then," April continued. "We all went to school, except for Meggie, who was only five. My father had his practice downtown, but my mother stayed home like the other women. They had maids back then, to help in the house, and the women gave canasta parties. That's what they did all day long: yell at their maids and play canasta."

August laughed, although he had no idea what canasta was. "Go on!" he urged her. "Then what happened?"

"Well, let's see," said April. "You know about my father. Mr. O'Malley owned a garage on Franklin

Street, and Mr. Todd was the manager of a bank downtown. That leaves Mr. Sweeny. None of us would be here now if it weren't for Mr. Sweeny."

"What did he do?" asked August.

"He was retired, and nobody knew what he did before. But the point is that Mr. Sweeny was worried about the war in Europe. He was afraid the United States would get involved, and he thought the first city to be bombed would be Baltimore. So he moved us."

"*He what?*" said August.

"He just up and moved us!" April giggled, remembering. "That was one night in October, and we were all asleep. When we woke up, Pineapple Place was in Phoenix, Arizona. He never asked us if we wanted to go, but it was too late to do anything about it. And we've been moving from one place to another ever since."

August felt dizzy at the idea. "Where else have you been?"

"Well, let's see. I didn't much like Phoenix—it got too hot. Mr. Sweeny thought so too, so he moved us to Missoula, Montana. That was nice, except the winters were too cold. Atlanta, Georgia, was pleasant, but there wasn't much to do there. And we all loved New Orleans so much that we've been there three times. Mr. Sweeny likes to keep us moving around, because he says it's the best way to learn geography. Don't you agree?"

August was too dazed to know if he agreed or not.

"We've lived in Georgetown before too," April continued, "way back when Dumbarton Oaks belonged to

Mr. Bliss. And we spent a year in Paris because Mr. Sweeny thought the twins lacked refinement—not that Paris helped, if you want my opinion. And after Paris was Kalamazoo, Michigan, and after Kalamazoo we came back here."

August was impressed. "I've lived only in Vermont and here," he said. "I bet there's no one in the whole world who has moved as much as you have!"

"And we're not through yet," April said proudly. "Mr. Sweeny wants to take us around the world. We haven't been to South America yet, or China. I don't know where we'll go next, but it's going to be soon. Mr. Sweeny is feeling poorly again, and that's a sure sign."

The thought of losing April just after he found her was so depressing that August stopped asking questions and agreed to play hide-and-seek.

It was the wildest game of hide-and-seek that August had ever played, because the children from Pineapple Place thought of the craziest ways to hide. When August was "it," he spent nearly an hour finding all the others. The twins were up a tree, Jessie and Meggie were clinging to the underside of the bridge, and April had covered herself with a heap of grass and fallen asleep under it.

Mike was the hardest. August spent twenty minutes combing the woods around the meadow. He might never have found Mike at all if April hadn't caught sight of him on the road outside the park.

"That's no fair!" cried August. "You're out of bounds!"

"Who cares?" said Mike. "Hide-and-seek is for babies!"

He scowled and shuffled his feet, and on the way back to the meadow he managed to bump into August and trip him. August knew he had done it on purpose. He hadn't really meant to fight with Mike, but before he knew it, they were rolling around on the path, shouting and hitting each other blindly.

"Stop it!" April screamed. "You stop it right this minute, both of you!"

But they didn't stop until Mike had given August a black eye and August had given Mike a bloody nose.

"Get up, you two!" April ordered them. "You ought to be ashamed of yourselves! There's blood on your chin, Mike, and look what you did to August's eye!"

August stood up and brushed the dirt off his pants. "Sorry, Mike!" he said. "You got me mad, that's all. But I can see how you feel about me. April told me everything. And I guess if you've been friends for half a century, you don't need any new people butting in. I guess I might as well go home."

To his surprise, Mike grinned. "I haven't had a good fight for forty-three years!" he told August. "You can't hit girls, and Jeremiah is too little, much as I'd like to give him a punch in the nose from time to time."

"Where *is* Jeremiah?" asked April. "He must be still hiding!"

They heard a self-satisfied laugh from a thick growth of underbrush nearby.

"I hear him, I hear him!" Meggie shouted. "I know where you are, Jeremiah!"

She ran toward the underbrush, and August grabbed her just in time.

"Don't go in there, you nitwit!" he said. "Can't you tell poison ivy when you see it?"

"Oh, no!" cried April, and the twins screamed with horror. Jeremiah had crawled into the largest patch of poison ivy August had ever seen, and was lying flat on his face right in the middle.

April, as usual, took charge of the situation. "You come out of there right now, Jeremiah, and don't touch anybody!"

Jeremiah crawled out, still looking immensely pleased with himself.

"Now march right down to the stream and take off all your clothes."

Jeremiah looked surprised, but he did what he was told. Meanwhile, April gathered an armful of meadow grass.

"It may not be too late," she said, "but if you don't watch out, Mrs. Sweeny is *really* going to have a case on her hands tomorrow!"

She made Jeremiah scrub himself all over with handfuls of grass. His face and body turned red as a boiled lobster, but he was shivering with cold and self-pity.

"April Anderson, I'm going to tell my mummy on you!" he wailed. "I'll catch the flu, you just see if I don't!"

"You'll prefer that to poison ivy, believe me," April said firmly. "And don't forget to scrub behind your ears."

When she decided that Jeremiah had scrubbed long and hard enough, she made him run around in the sun to warm up while she bundled his clothes inside her cardigan, being careful not to touch a thing that had been in the poison ivy. Then she told the twins to take off their sweaters too.

"Jeremiah can wear one on top and one on the bottom," she explained, "and he can just walk home barefoot. It serves him right!"

Jeremiah looked so funny dressed in that peculiar streaky wool from head to foot that August doubled up with laughter. This made Jeremiah cry again.

"I'm sorry!" August gasped. "Please don't take it personally!" And he laughed again, harder than ever.

The truth is that no one can wear an upside-down sweater for pants, even if it is a very dignified navy-blue sweater, without making people laugh, and the sweaters worn by the children from Pineapple Place were far from dignified. August kept looking to see what the people in the street would think as the children walked home, but no one turned around to stare.

"That's funny," he thought. "Jeremiah would never get away with it in Vermont!"

But cities were different. There were all kinds of crazy people walking around in cities, and maybe you got so used to them that you didn't even notice. That reminded him of something.

"You never told me about the rag-bag lady!"

"Yes I did," said April. "That's Mrs. Pettylittle."

"But what does she do? Why does she do it? Is she some kind of nut?"

April looked reproachfully at him. "She's not only not some kind of nut, she's the one who keeps the street alive. I don't know what we'd do without her. Of course, now she's teaching me and Mike to do it too so that if she ever gets sick or something, we could take over."

"Do what?" August asked impatiently. "Take over what?"

"She finds things for us," April explained. "She knows what we need, and she goes out on garbage days and brings it back to Pineapple Place. She's the only one of us who works outside, and everybody can see her. She's our link with civilization."

"Civilization?" August repeated. "In trash cans? But people don't throw things out unless they're no good any more!"

"Of course they don't," said April, "but that's where the rest of us come in. The grownups, I mean. They fix the things she brings home. Mrs. O'Malley patches the cloth together and makes our clothes. She's so good at it you'd never guess our things aren't new. And Mr. O'Malley repairs big things like refrigerators and our bicycles. Mr. Todd fixes all the little things like cups and plates, and he's good with furniture."

"And the others?" August asked.

"The others? Oh, they're busy doing other things. Mr. Sweeny organizes us, of course, and Mrs. Sweeny has her hands full taking care of Mr. Sweeny. My father is the doctor, and Mrs. Jenkins teaches us children reading and math and geography. We're naturally all very fond of geography."

"What about your mother?" August asked. "Is she the one who fixes up the food?"

"Food? Out of trash cans?" April turned up her nose in disgust. "Don't be ridiculous! Why, who knows what kind of germs we might catch? We buy our food at Fisher's Market, on Wisconsin Avenue."

August had never noticed Fisher's Market, but he thought it would be fun to shop for food there some day with April. Everything he did with April was fun. He hoped she would invite him to play again the next day.

As if she had read his thoughts April asked, "Can you come tomorrow?"

"I can come every day until school starts," said August, "and then I can come after school and on weekends."

"I don't know how much longer we're going to be here," said April, "but come tomorrow as early as you can."

The children from Pineapple Place offered to walk August home, but Jeremiah started to whine. "If I don't die of poison ivy, I'll die of pneumonia," he said, "and then you'll all be in trouble with my mummy!"

August suddenly caught sight of Michele, talking to some friends a block away. He called her name and waved.

"There's Michele!" he told April. "You take Jeremiah home, and I'll go back with her. I'll see you first thing in the morning."

But after he had gone a few yards he turned and ran back. "What about your mother?" he asked. "You never told me what your mother does."

"My mother? She knits, of course!" April looked proudly at her multicolored socks. "She gets the scraps of yarn from Mrs. Pettylittle and ties them end to end. There's not a sock or a sweater in Pineapple Place that she didn't make herself. And most of our blankets, and my party dress!"

August tried to think of something to say that wouldn't hurt her feelings. "Well," he said finally, "it certainly is a very unusual pattern!"

Then he turned and ran down the street to join Michele. "What did you think of them?" he asked excitedly when he caught up with her.

"Think of who?" asked Michele. "What happened to your eye?"

"Oh, nothing. Didn't you notice my friends from Pineapple Place?"

A funny expression passed over Michele's face. "I'm sorry, August, I thought you were alone. I guess I wasn't paying attention."

"But you must have noticed Jeremiah!" August protested. "The barefoot one who was wearing that weird sweater instead of pants."

Michele burst out laughing. "August Brown, what will you think up next?"

If Michele couldn't see the children from Pineapple Place, perhaps no one else could either. That explained why Jeremiah walked through the streets of Georgetown dressed in sweaters without attracting attention. But how humiliating to have people think he was making it all up!

Even his mother didn't believe him. After August had described the picnic, his fight with Mike O'Malley, and April's cure for poison ivy, she just said, "Do you think that's a safe place to go alone?"

"Alone!" August wailed. "What do you mean? There were eight of us!"

"All the same," said Mrs. Brown, "I would prefer you to stick to the places where other children play. And I wish you would tell the real story about how you got that black eye!"

"Why don't you believe me?" August demanded. "I always believe *you!*"

Mrs. Brown thought about it and smiled. "That's a good question, August. I think you deserve the benefit of the doubt. Why don't you invite April over to our house tomorrow for the day? That will settle the matter once and for all."

**6**

"I'm sorry," said April, "I'd love to come, but I'm afraid it won't work."

August looked gloomy. "Then my mother is going to think I'm telling lies."

"Hardly anyone ever sees us," April explained. "Or once in a while someone can see some of us but not others. It's unpredictable. But I don't mind trying."

Mr. Sweeny was still feeling poorly, and the children had been asked to play outside again. This time, however, August's mother had not packed him a picnic lunch. The children were walking down to N Street so that he could make himself a sandwich.

"You can share mine if you want," Mike had offered. "My mother always packs too much."

But August thought this would be a good excuse to introduce his mother to the children from Pineapple Place. He hated to have her think he was playing with imaginary friends.

"It won't work," April repeated. "You'll just be getting yourself deeper into trouble."

She refused to come inside because, she explained, although almost no one could see or hear the people from Pineapple Place except for Mrs. Pettylittle, everyone could feel them, and it isn't a pleasant feeling to bump into people you can't see.

"We'll stand outside your house," she promised. "Think of some reason to bring your mother to the window. But if I were you, I wouldn't say anything. Just wait and see what *she* says."

August's mother was still sitting at the breakfast table, reading the Sunday paper. "Did you ask April if she could come to play?" she asked.

"She doesn't want to," said August. "She couldn't come without the others, anyway, and I guess you wouldn't want eight kids in the house."

Mrs. Brown put down the paper and sighed. "August, I thought we decided to play this on the level."

"I am," August said crossly, "but you don't have to believe me unless you want to."

He spread peanut butter on one piece of bread, mayonnaise on another, and slapped the two together. His mother shuddered.

"How can you!" she protested. "Wouldn't you rather have tuna salad?"

"No thanks," said August, and he chose an apple from a bowl on the counter.

"Where are you going this time?" his mother asked.

"I don't know. Not far, though. Mrs. Sweeny said we could come back and play after Mr. Sweeny had his nap."

August put the apple and the sandwich in his jacket pockets. "Did you see the dead cat in the street?" he asked casually.

"Oh, no! How terrible!" his mother wailed. "Someone ought to take it and bury it!"

She ran to the living room window and looked out. August came up beside her.

"That's funny," said August. "It's gone now!"

April Anderson, Jeremiah Jenkins, and the five O'Malley children were standing in a row outside and waving. August watched his mother's face hopefully. At first she looked uninterested. Then she leaned forward and smiled.

"Oh, is that your friend April? She isn't a bit the way you described her."

"What do you mean?" asked August.

"Well, you said April was your age, didn't you? With brownish hair in ponytails? This girl couldn't be much over six, and she has bright red curls."

"That's Meggie O'Malley," said August. "She's only five. What about the others?"

"Other what?" his mother asked.

"Never mind," said August. He gave his mother a hug and ran to the front door.

"If that child is only five, she's much too young to be waiting in the street alone!" Mrs. Brown called after him.

When August joined the others on the sidewalk he hugged Meggie too. "You're 'it'!" he told her excitedly. "You win the jackpot, Miss Meggie O'Malley! My mother saw you!"

Meggie giggled. "You're silly!" she said. "Have you got your lunch? April says we can go rolling-and-bumping on the Georgetown campus."

April looked a little bit ashamed. "I don't think it's very nice," she said disapprovingly, "but they all love doing it—even Jeremiah—so I hate to say no. Those crazy O'Malleys invented the game."

August had already found out that the Georgetown University campus, only a few blocks from his house, was an excellent place to play. There were grassy lawns and winding cement walks, sheltered courtyards and terraces. The students never minded having children race about, and there were very few cars.

When they entered the main gates of the university, Mike O'Malley rushed to the middle of the circular driveway and climbed up on the statue of a seated man. From this vantage point he shouted at the students, sticking out his tongue and thumbing his nose.

"Can people hear him?" August asked.

"No, thank goodness!" April answered crossly. "That's John Carroll, the first archbishop of Baltimore. I don't think it's respectful to sit on an archbishop's lap, do you? And the O'Malleys are Catholic!"

She finally persuaded Mike to come down, and they started across the campus. August soon found out why Meggie had been so excited. Except for April, who, as she had said before, thought it must be an unpleasant feeling, the children from Pineapple Place considered knocking into people who couldn't see them the funniest thing in the world.

April walked with August, but the others ran zigzagging ahead, brushing shoulders with everyone who came toward them. The result was so funny that even April had to laugh. The students and teachers would turn and say, "Excuse me!" When they saw that they were all alone, they would look frightened and hurry away.

After a while the children came to the university playing field. This is a favorite spot for Georgetown children in winter because the field is closed in on three sides by steep slopes that are excellent for sledding. But the children from Pineapple Place preferred to come in warm weather because this was where they played the game called rolling-and-bumping.

The only rule for playing rolling-and-bumping is that you have to be invisible. In warm weather the slopes of the playing field are dotted with students talking and singing or even studying. The children from Pineapple Place would lie down at the top of the slope and roll faster and faster until they hurtled into the students, sending notebooks and guitars in all directions. When they reached the bottom of the slope, the children, whom the students never saw, would shriek with laughter, which the students never heard, and race uphill to begin again.

August was shocked. "Couldn't they give some warning?" he asked. "It's not fair if no one knows they're coming!"

"I think it's awful," April agreed, "but you have no idea how difficult it has been to keep six children happy day after day for forty-three years and more. I have to give in a bit, just for a little peace and quiet."

Rolling-and-bumping was not August's idea of peace and quiet, but he was glad to have a moment to talk with April. They unwrapped their sandwiches and lay down in the grass.

"I've been thinking," said April. "Your mother must be a very unusual person."

August's face clouded. "How should I know? She's gone all day, so I never get to see her any more."

"It's very rare for someone to notice us," April continued, "especially a grownup."

This made August feel proud, but he wasn't sure that his mother deserved it. "She only noticed Meggie," he pointed out, "and none of the rest of you. Anyway, she's been kind of funny lately."

"How?" asked April.

"Funny peculiar, ever since we left Vermont. I don't see why we had to leave in the first place. I mean, it's not as if my parents fought all the time. They were hardly ever in the house together, so why did they have to get a divorce? If we were still in Vermont, my mother wouldn't have to work and she'd be home more."

April thought about this. "She's home now," she observed, "but you didn't stay with her."

"Oh, well, that's different," said August.

"It's Sunday," said April. "She gets to see you only on weekends. She probably minds a lot."

August was furious. "But she leaves *me!*"

"That's what I mean," said April. "She lets you go

out even though she'd rather have you stay home, so you ought to let her go out too."

August had never before been preached at by a ten-year-old girl. He had noticed that April was bossy with the other children, but bossing August was another story.

"What makes you think you know all about it?" he asked angrily.

"I've been around for a long time," said April. She smiled at him. "I thought your mother looked awfully nice!"

"Well, I like yours too," August replied gruffly, "but I guess I'm going to roll."

He went as far away as possible from the other children so that no one would think he was responsible for the bumping. Then he rolled his mother out of his system.

When the bell in the clock tower tolled three, Jeremiah Jenkins came running up the slope, followed by the O'Malley children.

"It's time, it's time!" Jeremiah panted. "Can we go home now?"

August was surprised that the children wanted to abandon the game so suddenly, but April explained. "Mr. Sweeny's nap is over at three, so we can go back. And today is the day that Mr. Todd is finishing Jeremiah's roller skates."

Jeremiah was usually the slowpoke of the bunch. If he wasn't whining that the others went too fast, he was complaining about a stitch in his side, and if it wasn't a stitch in his side, it was a stone in his shoe. But today he raced ahead and didn't even look for cars.

"Jeremiah Jenkins!" April screamed. "You stop at the corner and wait for us! If a car hits you, you won't feel invisible, believe me, and we won't even be able to collect insurance!"

The children ran to Mr. Todd's house and rang the bell. A small, fussy-faced man with a mustache opened the door. He had a shiny bald patch on top of his head, and he wore glasses with pink translucent frames. He was dressed in gray from his bow tie down to a pair of old felt slippers, but underneath his dull gray jacket, August caught a glimpse of a multicolored knitted vest.

"So this is our new guest!" said Mr. Todd, looking at August. "Honored, I'm sure! Come in!"

He held the door wide open, and the children tramped into the living room.

Mr. Theophilus Todd himself might look gray, but his house was shiny and bright. The living room was crowded with chairs and coffee tables, bookcases and desks. Nothing matched, but everything was in perfect condition and polished to a gleam. There were curtains at every window and old prints on the wall. When August looked closely, he could see that the curtains had once been tattered, the prints torn, and the furniture broken in many places, but everything had been lovingly patched and mended.

The children from Pineapple Place were not interested in Mr. Todd's living room. They jumped up and down with excitement and all talked at once.

Mr. Todd motioned with his hands for them to be quiet, then turned to August.

"This is a big day in Pineapple Place," he told him with a twinkle in his eye. "I wonder if you can guess the reason?"

August already knew. He laughed when Jeremiah answered with a shout, "I get my new skates!"

Mr. Todd shuffled over to a cupboard. He took out a pair of roller skates and dangled them by the straps. They were clean and shiny, but they hardly looked new.

"It took me nearly a year to collect the parts for these," Mr. Todd told August. "It breaks my heart to make the children wait so long, but what can I do? It's the ball bearings that are so hard to find, although I suspect Mrs. Pettylittle doesn't know a ball bearing when she sees one. I would go out to look myself, but my arthritis slows me down. And garbage is so humid, you know. Very bad for arthritis."

His face was so sad as he said this that August felt sad too. "I guess it is a little damp," he agreed, remembering the disposable diapers.

Mr. Todd smiled again, however, when Meggie tugged at his jacket and squealed, "I'm next, aren't I, Mr. Todd? Now you can start mine!"

"Only the twins had roller skates when we were living back in Baltimore," Mr. Todd explained to August. "These other little monsters were after me for years to make them skates too. So one day I gave in, and we drew straws. Jeremiah came first, and then little Meggie here, although I'm afraid she's going to scrape her pretty little knees."

"Oh, no!" said Meggie with tears in her eyes.

Mr. Todd looked down at her affectionately. "Well, well, I wouldn't want to disappoint you. And next there's young Michael here to outfit, and then his sister Jessie."

"And I'm the last," said April mournfully, looking with envy at Jeremiah's skates. "I drew the shortest straw."

"But where do you skate?" August asked. "I have skates too, but the sidewalks are too bumpy in Georgetown and my mother won't let me skate in the street."

"Of course not!" said Tessie. "We skate on the tennis courts at Volta Park."

"But it hurts when the balls hit us," said Bessie, "so when we can, we go downtown. On nice days we skate on the mall, and when it rains we skate in the National Gallery."

"You mean the museum?" asked August. "I didn't know you could skate in there."

"*You* can't," the twins said smugly, "but *we* can."

Mr. Todd served lemonade and cookies, and then he offered to show August his collections. August could tell by a pleading look in April's eyes that he should accept.

"He hasn't had anyone new to show them to for forty-three years!" she whispered while Mr. Todd was pouring Meggie a second glass of lemonade. "We all know them by heart. Do you mind?"

August didn't mind because he was a collector himself. Mr. Todd led him from room to room, proudly pointing out the objects. "All those little boxes are made from matchsticks," he said. "It's extremely painstaking work. You would never dream the time it takes!"

He showed August a shoe box full of matchsticks, and August nodded appreciatively. He told Mr. Todd about his shoe box full of chicken wishbones.

"I don't know what you could make out of bones," said Mr. Todd. "Pencil stubs—now, I have my little plan for pencil stubs, when I have enough saved up."

After showing August his pencil stubs, he led him to a bookcase full of ships in bottles, all his own work, and then to a cupboard full of clocks.

"Twenty-nine clocks, all in perfect working order!" Mr. Todd boasted. "And every one of them was thrown away for lost. Actually, what you see there is fifty-nine clocks. I took them all apart and came up with these."

"What do you do with them?" August asked.

"Do? Nothing!" Mr. Todd shook his head sadly. "There's not a family on the street that doesn't have a clock of mine in every room, and sometimes several. I can't find any takers nowadays, but it's hard to give up an old habit. I don't suppose you could use a clock yourself now?"

August told him that he could. When he went home that evening, he was carrying a large alarm clock painted glossy pink with gold and silver flowers.

"It's for you!" he said, giving it to his mother.

Mrs. Brown was astonished. "For me? How lovely! Where on earth did you get it?"

"Mr. Todd made it," said August. "That's Mr. Theophilus Todd, who lives in—"

"Don't tell me. Let me guess," said Mrs. Brown. "He lives in Pineapple Place."

"That's right," said August, "and he made it out of—"

"Things he found in trash cans," his mother finished.

"No, Mrs. Pettylittle finds them," August corrected her. "Mr. Todd can't go rag-bagging because of his arthritis. Trash cans are too humid, he says."

Mrs. Brown sighed. "August, I love this clock, but there's something I want to talk to you about. I went for a walk while you were out. I walked on P Street, the whole way across Georgetown and the whole way back. And I'm sorry, but—"

"Don't say it!" August groaned.

His mother looked at his worried face and didn't say it.

**7**

At nine-thirty the next morning August was in the kitchen making a sandwich for lunch. He had just piled tuna salad on a slice of raisin bread and was about to add a layer of raspberry jam when he heard a loud knock. Licking his fingers, he ran to open the door and was astonished to find April on the front step, all alone.

"What would you have done if Michele had opened?" he demanded.

"Nothing," said April. "She couldn't see me, remember? So she wouldn't hear me knock."

"Where are the others?" August asked.

"Back home. They're waiting for us. We have to go out again today, but Mr. Sweeny wants to meet you first."

August had never seen April look so excited. Her cheeks were flushed, and she was stamping her feet with impatience.

"Where's your jacket? Hurry up! Mr. Sweeny doesn't like to wait. Have you got a comb? Oh, never mind, you can use mine."

"But I haven't finished making my sandwich!" August protested.

"Never mind your sandwich. We'll find you something to eat."

August ran inside to get his jacket and tell Michele where he was going. When he came out again, April was already hurrying down the street.

"Wait for me!" August shouted.

April grabbed his hand and pulled him after her, chattering excitedly, "This never happened before. I wonder what he wants! There's some jam on your cheek. Wipe it off. Can't you walk any faster?"

If it had been anybody else, August would have slowed down out of sheer contrariness, but he was too fond of April to hurt her feelings.

"He wasn't at all pleased when he heard how Mrs. Pettylittle brought you back for me," April continued. "He said it wasn't in the schedule, but I don't think he really minds. Zip up your jacket so he won't see those spots on your shirt!"

August was annoyed, but he zipped up his jacket.

April yanked August across O Street and dragged him after her up 35th. "Remember not to talk back, now. He likes to be called sir. Your shoelace is untied. Oh, I hope he doesn't take a dislike to you!"

This was too much for August. "So what if he does?"

April was flabbergasted. She stopped short in the middle of the sidewalk to stare at August. "Don't be foolish!" she whispered, as if Mr. Sweeny could over-

hear. "Oh, August, please don't try to show off or anything. He might never let you come back!"

August had always boasted that he was not afraid of
anything, but he certainly didn't want to be thrown out
of Pineapple Place. He let April wipe the jam off his
cheek and slick down his hair with her comb. And in
fact his stomach felt a little jumpy when she rang the
doorbell of the blue house with black shutters, especially when he noticed six anxious faces pressed to the
window of the house across the street.

At last the door opened and a dumpy gray-haired
woman dressed in white stood smiling at them. "Just on
time, April!" she said approvingly. "Mr. Sweeny will be
pleased. He does so like you children to be punctual!"

The children followed Mrs. Sweeny down a dark
corridor and stood quietly while she knocked at a closed
door. When a muffled voice called out from the other
side, Mrs. Sweeny opened the door and pushed them
both inside.

April held August's hand tighter than ever. "Don't
forget to say 'sir'!" she hissed.

The room was so dark that at first August saw no one
at all. Then he noticed a bundled-up shape in an armchair. When his eyes grew used to the dim light, he
realized that it was a man. Quite a fat old man with
white hair combed so carefully from ear to ear that
August could almost count the strands. A very self-
important old man with a stubborn-set mouth like a
nutcracker, and beady black eyes.

August was shocked to feel himself shivering. Out of self-respect, he dropped April's hand and forced himself to walk forward. "How do you do?" he asked boldly. "Sir!"

Mr. Sweeny scowled. "Proud as a peacock, it's clear to see. Boasting all over town that you got yourself invited to Pineapple Place. Well, it had nothing at all to do with you, and nothing to do with me!"

August's legs felt weak, but he didn't want April to see that he was afraid. He suddenly remembered one of the things his mother said in lawyer-talk.

"I understand that it's an unprecedented case," he told Mr. Sweeny, "and I considered myself—um—privileged. Sir."

Mr. Sweeny cleared his throat so noisily that it reminded August of the sea elephant at the National Zoo.

"And—" August added daringly, "I'm sorry you're sick."

Mr. Sweeny raised his eyebrows, grew purple in the face, and leaned as far forward in his armchair as his fat stomach and the blankets he was wrapped in would allow.

"Sick!" he shouted hoarsely. "Me, sick? I haven't been sick since I caught the flu back in 1947. I'm simply subject to chronic cyclical anticipatory motion discomfort."

August gasped. It sounded much worse than flu. He tried to think of something to say, but Mr. Sweeny interrupted his thoughts.

"Well, you needn't stand there gaping. What are you waiting for? I said I wanted to see you and I've seen you, so you can take yourselves off, the whole bunch of you, and don't come back until three o'clock. I need to think."

August was backing respectfully out of the room as if Mr. Sweeny were royalty, when to his surprise April ran forward and gave the fat old man a kiss.

"Oh, thank you! Thank you, Mr. Sweeny!" she cried breathlessly.

"Well now," Mr. Sweeny grumbled, "you're the only sensible one of the lot. Here, wait a minute."

With great difficulty he heaved his enormous body to one side and fumbled in his trousers pocket. "Show your friend around the town," he said, giving April a handful of coins. "Buy him an ice-cream cone, take him on the streetcar, pay him a ride on the carousel! Enjoy yourselves! But keep those O'Malley brats out of trouble. I don't know what the younger generation is coming to! Hardly worth saving—I might as well move the whole street back to Baltimore and let the bombs fall where they will."

After this confusing speech, Mr. Sweeny sighed noisily, closed his eyes, and seemed to go to sleep. April and August tiptoed to the door, but before they had left the room, Mr. Sweeny's eyes flew open and he roared after them, "And don't forget, I want you back here not one minute after three!"

Jeremiah and the O'Malley children were waiting

outside. They were very solemn-faced, and when April and August joined them, Jeremiah asked in a frightened voice, "What did Mr. Sweeny do to August?"

Once August was out of that dark room, he forgot his fears. "Nothing, of course!" he scoffed. "Who's afraid of a fat old man?"

But April said, "Hush, August! He was very nice to you, and just look!"

She held out a fistful of coins. "He said to take the streetcar to the carousel!"

The children bustled together excitedly. They counted the money several times over, and Jessie O'Malley had a fierce argument with Jeremiah Jenkins over whether peanuts or doughnuts should be bought with the spare change. April settled the matter by slipping the coins into her skirt pocket.

"Mr. Sweeny gave the money to *me,*" she said, "so it's for me to spend. And there won't *be* any spare change if you go on fighting!"

August saw six faces grow cloudy and six mouths open to protest. He decided to change the subject. "Where's this streetcar?" he asked. "My mother and I always take the bus."

"We can't take the bus," April explained, "because buses are crowded, and it bothers people to see a big empty space in the aisle that they can't push through. The last time we tried, a woman started screaming, and they had to stop the bus and make everybody get off."

"Streetcars are more fun, anyway," said Mike O'Malley. "They're open-sided in warm weather, and they're much bumpier!"

August could tell by the look on Mike's face that the bumpier a streetcar was, the more fun it was.

But suddenly Mike's face fell. "We can't take August on a streetcar," he pointed out. "Streetcars aren't *now.*"

"I don't understand," said August. "If streetcars aren't now, how can you ride on them?"

"It's different for us," April explained. "Sometimes we're *now,* and sometimes we're *then.* We go back and forth. I wonder if Mr. Sweeny is arranging for you to come back to *then* with us, just for today?"

Mike shook his head doubtfully. "Even Mr. Sweeny can't do that," he said.

"Who knows?" said April. "Let's find out!"

When August walked out of Pineapple Place that morning, things looked different. It was the same balmy spring day, there still were birds singing in the trees and flowers growing outside the houses, but many of the houses were painted different colors. There weren't as many cars in the street, and what cars there were looked old-fashioned. Instead of stopping at 35th Street, the old streetcar rails on P Street intersected new rails that August had never seen before. Sugar's Drugstore looked different, and the weaving shop around the corner from August's house was gone; in its place was a restaurant. August's house itself was shabbier, and painted an unfamiliar yellow. August wanted to knock at the door and see if Michele was there, but April was in a hurry.

The children walked downhill to M Street, where they turned left and headed for Wisconsin Avenue. Now things looked stranger than ever. There were lots of those old-fashioned cars driving past or parked outside the stores. A streetcar clanged its bell and jolted by.

August recognized some of the stores, but many others were new. Brewton's Office Supplies Store was still there, and so was Meenehan's Hardware, but instead of the usual flowerpots and barbecue sets, there were a bear trap and a cluster of milking cans in Meenehan's display windows.

August wanted to stop and look at the bear trap, but April tugged his sleeve impatiently. "We haven't got all day!" she said.

August was so fascinated by the unfamiliar stores that he didn't look where he was going and stumbled several times. There were wonderful country smells coming from a store marked P. T. Moran, which sold farm supplies. There was a horse on the sidewalk outside another store called Stombock's. At first August thought it was real, but it was only stuffed. The children stopped to stroke the glossy hide.

"They bring him out for the day and take him in at night," Mike told August, "just like a real horse. I tried to ride him once, but they made me get down. They can see us."

August began to shiver with excitement. At last he understood. He wasn't *now* any more, he was back *then* with the children from Pineapple Place, years before he was born. Mr. Sweeny had arranged it after all!

April led him up Wisconsin Avenue, holding his hand to keep him from tripping because August's eyes were everywhere but on his feet. He noticed more streetcar rails, and far away at the top of the hill he could see another streetcar. Then, to his delight, a hansom cab rolled by.

"Watch where you're going!" April said sharply as August bumped into a street lamp.

It hurt, but he hardly noticed. The children from Pineapple Place were filing into a grocery store that August was sure did not exist in *now*. So this was Fisher's Market, where April's mother bought her food! It smelled better than the supermarket where August's mother shopped. August could smell fruit and earthy vegetables and cool, fresh meat. He watched while April bought some sliced ham, a hunk of cheddar cheese, eight oranges, and an unsliced loaf of bread.

When they were out in the street again, she turned anxiously to August. "Well? Have you noticed anything different?"

"Anything different!" August exploded. "Do you think I'm blind? It's *all* different!"

"Hurray for Mr. Sweeny!" Mike shouted. "He let August come to *then*—now we can take him on the streetcar!"

August had never been on a streetcar before, and he soon agreed with Mike that it was more exciting than a bus. The eight children squeezed into two benches, with August on the outside of one because it was his first time, and Mike on the outside of the other because he got there first and refused to budge.

The streetcar jolted across Georgetown, stopping now and then with a squeal of its wheels and a clang of its bell, to let passengers climb on and off. A warm wind sent the children's hair flying around their faces and blew a cherry blossom into Jessie's mouth. She had a fit of coughing, mixed with giggles. It seemed odd to see other people smile at the children from Pineapple Place and even speak to them; August was used to their being invisible to everyone but himself.

The streetcar headed straight along P Street until it reached 35th Street. Then it turned downhill for a few blocks before swinging to the right again at Prospect Street. From there on it traveled west, above the C and

O Canal, leaving the spires of Georgetown University far behind as it moved into the country.

Trees and flowers were everywhere. Once in a while August caught a glimpse of the canal or even, farther below and farther away, the Potomac River. He was half-hypnotized with delight, and could hardly bear it when the car stopped at Glen Echo Park and the children crowded off.

"Never mind," April said when she saw his face. "The carousel is even better, and after that you have the ride home."

The carousel was inside a big gray building at the top of a hill. As the children hurried up the road, August wondered if it would be much different from the merry-go-rounds at county fairs back in Vermont. They were fun, but nothing special.

Soon he heard music playing, wild and gay and a little jerky. At the sound of the music, the children from Pineapple Place broke into a run, laughing and shouting as they drew near the top of the hill. Just as they reached the building, the music stopped.

"Hurray!" they shouted. "We're just on time!"

The carousel was painted with warm, bright colors. There were lights and mirrors under the roof, and more around the central core. August was used to merry-go-rounds with horses, but this one seemed to have all the animals of the ark. The twins each mounted a prancing horse, and Jessie climbed up on a zebra. Meggie straddled an alligator, while Jeremiah made a dash for the leopard. Mike O'Malley hesitated between a lion and a tiger and finally chose the tiger. April sat high on the back of a giraffe. August had such a hard time making up his mind that when the music started and the carousel began to move, he was still standing on the platform. He quickly climbed on the nearest thing, which happened to be an ostrich.

Only a few minutes earlier he had thought that nothing could be more fun than a streetcar ride, but August's first ride on the carousel was the most glorious thing that had happened to him in his whole life. At first the carousel moved heavily, as if it couldn't work up speed. Then it seemed to lighten, and moved a little faster. Before long it was turning so fast that the children stopped waving to one another and held on with both hands. Meggie squealed, and the twins began to laugh hysterically. The animals rose up and down like the swell of the sea. Now and then the carousel would jerk and August would think it was about to stop, but it kept on spinning faster and faster, until the children were caught up in a dizzy whirlwind of mirrors, lights, and music.

When it was over, August was too dazed to move. He sat dreamily with his hot cheek pressed against the cool paint of the ostrich's neck, until April came and helped him down.

"I have enough money for one more ride apiece," she told him. "But let's have lunch first and keep the best for last."

They found a picnic table in the sun and spread out

the purchases from Fisher's Market. April borrowed Mike O'Malley's pocketknife and cut the loaf of bread into eight huge slices. She cut the cheese into eight parts too, and divided up the ham. Then she gave each child an orange.

They didn't talk much while they ate. The sun was very warm, and they still felt a little dizzy. Meggie's eyelids drooped, and she laid her head down on her arms. After a while Jeremiah stretched out on the grass and went to sleep with a half-chewed piece of bread sticking out of his mouth. April sat lazily humming the tune the carousel had played. August hoped she would remember the second ride, but she was in no hurry. Meggie and Jeremiah had been asleep for close to an hour before she stood up and dealt out the rest of Mr. Sweeny's coins.

The second ride on the carousel was as good as the first, and every bit as long. By the time the children had gathered themselves together and started down the road, the air was cooler and the shadows were lengthening.

They waited a long time for the streetcar. Clouds began to gather overhead. Meggie complained that she was feeling chilly, and August made her put on his jacket. Jeremiah started whining that his feet hurt and he felt like being sick.

"I wonder what's wrong?" Mike said. "We've never had to wait this long before!"

Just then a woman walked by, pushing a baby carriage. When Mike ran up and asked if she knew why the streetcar was delayed, the woman looked right through him and nearly ran into him with the carriage.

"That's odd!" said Mike. "I don't think she can see me. You try, August."

When August spoke to her the woman stopped. "Can you tell me when the next streetcar is coming?" August asked.

The woman stared at him as if he were insane. "Streetcar? What streetcar?" she said. "There haven't been streetcars running out here for years! Where do you want to go?"

"Back to Georgetown," August replied.

"Then take a bus," the woman advised him, pushing the baby carriage ahead again. "The N-4 and N-5 go back into town."

April's face turned pale. "We must be back in *now!*" she said. "Quick, ask her what time it is!"

August asked and the woman looked at her watch. "It's a quarter to four," she told him.

August couldn't understand why the children from Pineapple Place were so upset. "What does it matter?" he asked. "Let's take the bus."

"Don't you remember what I told you? We *can't* take buses!" April wailed. "Oh, why didn't I listen to Mr. Sweeny? He *said* to be back by three o'clock!"

Mike was kicking the old streetcar rail furiously. "He did it on purpose to trick us," he grumbled. "He must have done it for a joke, and it's not funny!"

August thought hard. "I could take the bus home and talk to Mr. Sweeny," he suggested. "Maybe if I asked nicely, he would switch the rest of you back to *then* again."

But the younger children were cold and tired.

"We'd better start walking," said April. "We won't get anywhere standing here and complaining."

It had taken a long time for the streetcar to reach Glen Echo Park. August suspected that if they walked back to Georgetown, they might be walking all night, but he set off down the street with the children from Pineapple Place. After a few blocks, however, Jeremiah sat down on the curb and began to cry.

"You baby!" April scolded him. "If Meggie can do it, you can. You're two years older than she is!"

But for once Jeremiah had a good reason to cry: he pulled off his shoes and socks and showed April two enormous blisters on his heels.

Now even April felt discouraged. She didn't dare take the bus, and they couldn't afford a taxi. She and August and the twins took turns carrying Jeremiah, but that only slowed them down, and it was growing colder. When they passed a public telephone, August had an idea.

"I know!" he cried. "I'll telephone my mother. She can come and pick us up."

August was glad that his mother had made him memorize her number at work. He dialed it quickly and told the secretary that it was an emergency. When his mother came to the phone, she sounded frightened.

"What's the matter? Have you hurt yourself?"

After August reassured her, she was angry, not relieved. "Glen Echo Park! But that's way out in the suburbs! How on earth did you get there?"

August started to tell about Mr. Sweeny and the streetcar, but his mother cut him short.

"You can save your story for the ride back home," she said angrily, "and you'd better make it good: you have a lot of explaining to do!"

The wait for Mrs. Brown seemed endless. The sky grew darker, and the spring breeze turned into an icy winter wind. It began to drizzle, and the three younger children were in tears. At last the car drew up, and August's mother leaned over to open the door. She looked very cross.

"You sit in front, August," she ordered, "and Meggie can go in back. It's just as well there aren't eight of you, although I would be happier if you had told the truth for once."

August looked with dismay at the seven children from Pineapple Place: the back seat was meant for only two!

"I can sit on someone's lap," Meggie offered.

Mrs. Brown raised her eyebrows. "Whatever for? You have the whole back seat to yourself. Now, hop in and I'll turn the heat on. Your clothes are wet, and you're shivering. What can your parents be thinking of, letting you go off like this by yourself?"

As usual, April solved the problem. "Jeremiah, you sit on Bessie's lap and Jessie can sit on Tessie's. Mike and I will share that hump in the middle, and Meggie will just have to squeeze in next to the window. She can't sit on anyone's lap or it will look as if she's floating, and August's mother might get scared and have an accident."

August's mother did not hear a word of these instructions. After Meggie climbed in, she reached over and slammed the door, barely missing the last foot to be pulled inside, which happened to be Jeremiah's.

The back seat was so crowded that August could not tell who was on whose lap. It was one big jumble of arms and legs, wet clothes, and dripping hair. As the car grew warmer, the wet clothes began to steam, and soon there was a strong smell of damp wool that August suspected came from Mrs. Anderson's peculiar socks and sweaters.

Mrs. Brown sniffed once or twice with a puzzled look on her face. Then she glanced around and noticed Meggie.

"You silly child!" she cried. "Why are you sitting all scrunched up like that? Move into the middle of the seat and get comfortable!"

There were loud squeals of protest as Meggie pushed her way toward the middle of the seat. The children were shoving and complaining so loudly that August could hardly believe his mother didn't hear them. To make things worse, the twins screamed every time Mrs. Brown drove around a curve.

August could stand it no longer. He turned and shouted at them, "Do you mind!"

Mrs. Brown was astonished. "How can you be so rude to Meggie? She was so quiet back there that I thought she was asleep!"

Meggie smiled sweetly at her. "It's so much fun!" she said. "This is the first time we've been in an automobile for forty-three years!"

Mrs. Brown frowned and gripped the steering wheel so tightly that her knuckles turned white. Her lips were pursed, and she didn't say another word until she reached Georgetown. Then she asked, "Where do you live, Meggie? I'm taking you straight home to put on some dry clothes."

"I live at number six, Pineapple Place," said Meggie.

Mrs. Brown's voice had the low, controlled sound to it that August knew meant trouble: "I'm afraid I don't know where that is, Meggie. You'll have to tell me which way to go."

Meggie directed her down 34th Street and right on P Street. Half a block farther on, she asked her to stop.

"Here?" said Mrs. Brown. "Are you sure?"

Meggie thanked Mrs. Brown politely and opened the car door. April, Jeremiah, and the older O'Malley children tumbled out noisily, but Mrs. Brown caught Meggie's wrist.

"Wait a moment, young lady. This game has gone far enough! I don't see any Pineapple Place, and I'm not going to leave you in the middle of the street. So either you tell me your real address or you come home with us until someone comes to claim you."

Instead of protesting, Meggie smiled happily. "Oh, goody!" she cried. "I always wanted to see August's house, but April never lets us go inside."

August's mother sighed with annoyance. She drove back down to N Street, parked the car, and, holding Meggie by the elbow in case she tried to run away, led her inside the house. Then she shooed both children up to August's room.

"Take off those wet clothes," she said, "and, August, you find Meggie some warm socks and give her one of your shirts—she can roll up the sleeves and wear it as a dress. And then come downstairs. I want to talk to you!"

When August came back down, followed by Meggie in his blue plaid flannel shirt, his mother had set out two mugs of hot chocolate and a plate of cookies. She stood in front of them while they ate and told them exactly what she thought of children who let their imaginations run wild and end up making total nuisances of themselves.

"And what a five-year-old child is doing in the streets alone, I can't imagine," she finished angrily, "but your parents ought to be reported to the authorities, and if you don't give me your real address immediately, I shall be forced to call the police."

Meggie smiled innocently and took another cookie.

"Very well," said Mrs. Brown, and she reached for the telephone.

Just then there was a sharp knock at the door. Mrs.

Brown put the receiver on the hook and went to see who it was. She came back with a confused look on her face, followed by Mrs. Pettylittle.

"I've come to fetch Meggie back home," Mrs. Pettylittle explained. "You were so kind to bring all those naughty children home in your car!"

She and Meggie were out the door and walking down the street before August's mother recovered from her surprise. "But that's the bag lady!" she cried. "Is she Meggie's mother?"

"Of course not," said August. "That's Mrs. Pettylittle. They must have sent her because she's the only one you can see."

"Nonsense!" said his mother. "Why was she in such a hurry? I never gave her Meggie's clothes!"

She looked at the sodden mass that August had dumped on the kitchen floor. Then she bent down and picked up Meggie's sweater, holding it gingerly by the sleeve.

"What a ridiculous piece of knitting!" she exclaimed. "Who could have gone to so much trouble for such a silly result?"

August felt that he had done enough explaining for one day, especially since his mother didn't believe a word he said. Besides, he had a question of his own. "Mr. Sweeny has chronic cyclical anticipatory motion discomfort," he said. "Is that catching?"

To his surprise, his mother threw back her head and laughed. "It's just a pretentious way of saying that he always feels sick before he travels," she explained when she could keep a straight face. "Why? Where is he going?"

"Nowhere, I hope," said August. But he remembered what April had said about Pineapple Place moving again soon, and he had a sinking feeling that it might be true.

August slept later than usual the next morning. Even before he opened his eyes, he knew that it was still raining, because the cars made a swishing noise in the street below. The sky was dark, and little drops hung trembling from the branch outside his window.

For once August was in no hurry to get up; his head ached, and his throat felt funny when he swallowed. He lay there swallowing experimentally to see if it was a painful feeling or not, but he couldn't make up his mind. Then he looked at the clock. Eight-thirty! He tumbled out of bed and ran downstairs.

Michele was sitting cross-legged on the living room sofa, watching television. She waved at August but didn't take her eyes off the set.

"Your mother left for work already," she said. "Just wait for the commercial and I'll fix you some eggs."

"I don't want eggs," said August.

He went into the kitchen, put two slices of bread in the toaster, and filled a bowl with cornflakes and milk. The cornflakes hurt when he swallowed. He put the bowl aside and tried the toast, but that felt scratchy too. August ate two bites and decided that he wasn't hungry after all. When Michele came into the kitchen, he was slouched over the table, staring moodily at the toaster, his head in his hands.

"Sure you don't want eggs?" Michele asked.

"No!" said August gruffly.

"*No,* you don't want eggs or, *no,* you're not sure?" Michele looked at the cold toast and the bowl of soggy cereal. "What's the matter? Feel sick?"

"I don't know. Maybe I'm getting a cold," said August. "My throat feels kind of funny."

"Well, it's a perfect day to stay home," said Michele. "Who needs to go out in the rain? Let's watch TV."

"Soap operas?" August said scornfully. "No thanks!"

He went to the window seat in the living room and looked out at the street. The pavement was wet and shiny. People walked by holding umbrellas. The bulging black plastic garbage bags on the sidewalk were studded with glistening drops of water.

Suddenly August remembered. It was Tuesday—garbage day again! He wondered whether Mrs. Pettylittle minded rag-bagging in the rain, and he peered up and down the street to see if she was already at work. A few yards away, half in and half out of a trash can, he saw not Mrs. Pettylittle but Mike O'Malley! August forgot the feeling in his throat and ran for his jacket. Cold or no cold, he wasn't going to miss a chance to rag-bag!

Michele frowned, but she didn't take her eyes from the television screen. "If you have a cold, you'd better not go out in the rain!" she said after the exciting part was over. But by that time August was gone.

Mike O'Malley grinned when he saw August. "I was hoping you'd notice me," he said. "That's why I chose your street to work on. We're not allowed to play today because we're being punished for getting home late yesterday. We have to rag-bag instead. But I can't help it if you follow me around, can I?"

August thought that rag-bagging looked like fun, not punishment. He hoped that Mike would let him help. "Where's April?" he asked. "Is she rag-bagging too?"

"We all are," said Mike. "The others are just around the corner. Mr. Sweeny said we have to help Mrs. Pettylittle until the trucks come, and then we have to do lessons, even though it's spring vacation. Mrs. Jenkins is furious. She says there's no reason she should get punished too."

Mike gave August a shopping bag. Rag-bagging was mainly a matter of imagination, he explained. You had to keep in mind what you needed and imagine how the things you found in the trash would help.

"Take our roller skates," he said. "There's one chance in a million you'll find a pair of skates. But if you imagine skates while you're rag-bagging, you notice things that might be useful, like wheels and bits of metal and even shoelaces."

"What are you keeping in mind today?" August asked.

"Well, skates, of course," said Mike. "That's become a habit. But today Mrs. Pettylittle said to think spring."

"Think spring!" August repeated. "How do you do that?" He shivered as a drop of rain rolled down inside his collar. His hands felt clammy, and he put them in his pockets.

"Come with me," said Mike. "I'll show you what we've collected so far."

Among them the seven children from Pineapple Place had collected seven bags full of what looked like junk to August. He couldn't understand why April was so pleased with herself when she found a filthy gardening glove with a torn thumb, or why Meggie screamed with delight when she discovered a rusty trowel with a broken handle.

August tried hard to think spring, but it only made his headache worse, and all he could find to put in his shopping bag was an old sneaker.

April noticed that he was looking discouraged. "Never mind," she said. "It takes practice. Why not think roller skates instead? You might bring us luck."

August went three blocks up 34th Street and half a block east on Volta Place, thinking roller skates as hard as he could. Then he looked up and saw a street sign.

"Hey, this is Pomander Walk!" he cried. "This used to be my favorite street in Georgetown before I found Pineapple Place. Have you ever rag-bagged in here?"

Pomander Walk is a quiet, dead-end lane across from Volta Park. There are only ten houses, five on each side of the street, and it is one of the prettiest spots in Georgetown, but when you walk by on Volta Place, you would never guess it was there.

The children from Pineapple Place were not interested in rag-bagging in Pomander Walk. "Those people
are too neat and clean," said April. "They never throw
away anything worthwhile."

"I'll give it a try anyway," said August. "Wait for me
—I'll be right back."

There was a trash can in front of each of the ten little
houses. The first nine cans held nothing but trash, but
in the tenth August found a roller skate. It was missing
one wheel and the toe guard, but it was still a roller
skate. When the children saw it, they screamed with
excitement, passing it from hand to hand.

Meggie, who was next on the list for skates, threw her
arms around August and kissed him. "No one ever
found a whole skate before!" she cried. "You're an even
better rag-bagger than Mrs. Pettylittle!"

After August found the skate, rag-bagging lost some
of its interest. No more treasures were found in trash
cans, and the younger children began to fuss.

"Let's go home now," April said when they reached
Dent Place. "We've done well enough, and Mrs. Pettylittle likes to do this street herself."

Mike O'Malley began to laugh. "Wouldn't it be
funny if we put something in a can to scare her!" he said.

"Like what?" August asked.

"Oh, I don't know," said Mike. "Like one of us, for
instance. I could hide in an empty can and pop out and
scream."

Judging by his morning's work, August could think
of more agreeable places to hide than in a trash can, but

the children from Pineapple Place howled with laughter and began to squabble over who should hide. Bessie reminded the others that she was the oldest by seventeen minutes, but Mike argued that he thought of the idea in the first place. Then Jeremiah started to cry and insisted that he should be the one to hide because he wanted to the most. The other children stopped arguing and stared at him in disgust.

April said, "Why not? A trash can is the best place I can think of for a crybaby, and at least the rest of us will have a peaceful walk home."

They dumped the contents of a large trash can into several others and helped Jeremiah to climb inside.

"Now remember, when Mrs. Pettylittle lifts off the lid, you jump up and scream!" Mike instructed him. "Quick, get your head down—she just came around the corner!"

Laughing, the children ran down the street, waving at Mrs. Pettylittle as they passed her.

"Isn't it nasty weather?" she called after them. "You'd better hurry along home. Mrs. Jenkins is waiting for you."

August left the others at the corner of P Street. It was only ten o'clock in the morning, but his head ached worse than ever, and his throat felt as if he had swallowed a wad of sandpaper.

Michele scolded him when he came indoors. "You're soaked through again, just like yesterday!" she cried. "You've got to be crazy!"

August changed his clothes and let Michele dry his

hair with her hair dryer. He even agreed to wrap up in a blanket on the sofa and take his temperature, and he wasn't a bit surprised when Michele looked at the thermometer and shrieked, "A hundred and four! I'd better call your mom."

Mrs. Brown told Michele that she was coming straight home to drive August to the doctor. While they were talking, August heard the garbage truck working its way along the street. He picked up the blanket and moved to the window seat to watch. Just as the truck pulled up outside his house, he saw April running toward him on the sidewalk. She signaled wildly and he hurried to open the door.

"What's the matter?" he asked. "You look awful!"

April's face was pale, and she had been crying. "Oh, August! Mrs. Pettylittle never found Jeremiah! She didn't do Dent Place after all because of the rain, and Jeremiah never came home, and now the truck has gone by, and I'm afraid they took him to the dump!"

August looked at the truck outside his house. The men had tossed in half a dozen plastic garbage bags, and now the heavy steel blade was closing down and crushing the bags inward to the front of the truck. He shuddered at the thought of that happening to Jeremiah.

"Are you sure?" he asked. "He might be hiding. Let's go look!"

Still wrapped in his blanket, August followed April up the hill toward Dent Place. The street was over five blocks away, and the rain was falling steadily now.

August felt miserable, but he knew that he couldn't go home until Jeremiah was found.

April was right. The truck had passed, and the trash cans stood empty on the sidewalk. Jeremiah was nowhere to be seen. They called his name up and down the street, but no one answered.

"It's no use," April moaned. "Let's go back to Pineapple Place. Will you come too? I'm afraid to go alone!" Tears were streaming down her cheeks, and when she wiped them away with her sleeve, her cheeks became smudged with dirt.

August felt sorry for her. As they turned into Pineapple Place, he reached out from his blanket and held April's hand. "It's as much my fault as yours," he said. "We were all to blame. The only thing I can't understand is, why didn't Jeremiah yell or something? He's not the type to suffer in silence. In fact, he's the complainingest person I know!"

"No one would hear him if he yelled," April reminded him. "You keep forgetting! No one would hear him and no one would see him."

Suddenly April's face brightened. "No one would see him!" she repeated. "Jeremiah *can't* be in a garbage truck! That can would look empty to the men, so they wouldn't have any reason to dump it!"

April ran into the blue house with yellow shutters, pulling August after her. There, sitting at one of seven desks in Mrs. Jenkins's living room and looking very smug, was Jeremiah.

Mrs. Jenkins was a thin woman with dark hair pulled

back in a bun and a prim little pursed-up mouth. She had a long, thin nose that turned up at the tip, and the tip was pinker than the rest. August thought she would be an unpleasant-looking woman if she did not have Jeremiah's big blue eyes and long lashes. No matter how silly those eyes looked in Jeremiah's face, they were very pretty in his mother's.

August smiled at her. "I'm awfully sorry about what happened, Mrs. Jenkins," he said.

Mrs. Jenkins looked surprised, but she smiled back. "Why, there's no harm done," she said. "It was naughty of the older children to make Jeremiah soil his clothes. They're perpetually teasing the poor little thing, and he has such a sensitive nature! But I'm sure it wasn't your fault."

August wondered if she knew what really happened, but he certainly wasn't going to tell her. Jeremiah had probably already done his best to get the others into trouble.

Mrs. Jenkins handed April a textbook and told her to sit down. "You're doing American history with Michael O'Malley," she said. "The twins are memorizing a passage from 'The Song of Hiawatha,' and the little ones are working on their times tables."

"Except for me," said Meggie, smiling up at August. "I'm practicing capital *B*'s."

Mrs. Jenkins offered to find August a chair and another textbook, but he refused politely. He never would have thought he'd rather go to bed than be with the children from Pineapple Place, but such was the case today. He hurried home as fast as his aching throat would allow and collapsed on the sofa. He made no objection to being driven to Doctor Schultz, and didn't have the energy to protest when his mother complained bitterly about him to the doctor after the examination.

"I come home and find him wrapped in a wet blanket, soaked to the bone for the third time in two days, with a temperature of a hundred and four!" said Mrs. Brown. "I haven't had a word of back-talk from him in days, and he seems happy, but he's involved in some ridiculous game about invisible children, and I'm afraid he's beginning to believe it himself! Do you think there's something wrong with him?"

Doctor Schultz was a comfortable-looking woman, much older than August's mother. She leaned back in her chair and smiled at August. "The only thing I can see is a touch of flu," she told him. "You'll be all right if you rest for a day or two and take the medicine I prescribed. Now, tell me about those invisible children."

"They're not invisible!" August protested. "Not to me, anyway."

Doctor Schultz nodded in an understanding way. "It's quite normal to create imaginary friends," she told August. "You'd be surprised how many children invent playmates that only they can see."

August liked Doctor Schultz, but he felt exhausted and extremely cross. "They're just as real as you are!" he shouted hoarsely. "Am I inventing you just now? You'd better watch out or I'll *uninvent* you!"

Mrs. Brown stood up quickly, said good-by, and hurried August out of the office. "Where are your manners?" she scolded. "What would your father say if he heard you talk that way?"

"Let's move back to Vermont and find out," said August.

Mrs. Brown sighed. "You know we can't go back, August. We've discussed this before. But it upsets me that you're unhappy enough to invent an imaginary world."

"Those people are real," August said as he climbed into the back seat of the car. "Someday I'll prove it to you."

But before he could think of a way to do it, he fell asleep.

It rained all day Wednesday. August slept late and felt so much better when he woke up that he moved downstairs to the window seat. There was not much to see in the street. People hurried past, half-hidden under umbrellas. The postman came by on his rounds, stamping up and down the steps of each house and rattling the mail slots. August hoped there would be a letter from Zachary Judge, but there were only bills and catalogues for his mother. He also hoped that April would come to see what had happened to him, but there was not a sign of her all day long.

"What a waste of time!" he complained to his mother that evening. "Now I only have four days left before school starts."

His mother laughed. "A week ago you were so bored that you didn't know what to do with yourself!"

"That was before I found Pineapple Place," said August. "Can I go out tomorrow? I feel terrific—I really do!"

"That depends on the weather," said Mrs. Brown, "and on how your throat feels in the morning."

August's throat felt fine the next morning, but the rain was falling as steadily as ever. His mother not only refused to let him go to Pineapple Place but would not even allow him to stay at home, because Michele had caught August's cold and was spending the day in bed.

"You're coming to the office with me today," Mrs. Brown said firmly. "That way Michele can get some rest, and I'll be sure you stay out of trouble."

"Can't I go to April's house?" August begged. "We'll stay inside all day, I promise!"

Mrs. Brown had tried not to mention Pineapple Place since the trip to Doctor Schultz, but she could hardly avoid it now. "I know I said I'd give you the benefit of the doubt," she said crossly, "but I refuse to let you spend the day at a house I can't see, especially when it's pouring rain where the house is supposed to be. And that's that!"

Mrs. Brown's office was in downtown Washington, D.C., not far from the Mall. August had gone there on the bus one day with Michele. That had been fun, but his mother's office was definitely *not* August's idea of fun. It was crowded with file cabinets and stacks of folders, and even the magazines in the waiting room all dealt with legal matters.

August took his baseball cards, his rubber-band collection, and a library book to read, but he suspected that he would be bored, and he was right. It turned out he had already read the book, and he knew all the facts on the baseball cards by heart. He offered to show his cards to the receptionist, but she was too busy. So he sat in the waiting room sorting his rubber bands, first by size, then by color, and wondering if he could persuade his mother to take him to McDonald's for lunch.

Every few minutes someone would come into the office. Once it was the United Parcel man, and several times secretaries came in from other offices. August invented a game. He tried to guess whether the next visitor would be a man or a woman. If he was wrong, he had to pay one baseball card, but if he was right, he got a card back. When all the cards were gone, he would lose the game. By eleven o'clock he had lost all but one of his cards. He guessed that the next person through the door would be a man, but he was wrong again. The next visitor was April Anderson.

"How did *you* get here?" August shouted happily.

The receptionist looked up in surprise. "I beg your pardon?" she said.

"Don't talk!" April warned him. "Let me do the talking. We went to see if you could play, but you didn't come to the door no matter how hard I knocked. So I got Mrs. Pettylittle to ask your sitter where you were, and she gave us this address. Can you come out and play?"

August looked glum and shook his head.

"Why not? Are you being punished?" April asked.

August shrugged.

"We're going to the National Gallery to let Jeremiah

try his new skates," said April. "It'll be fun—you wait and see!"

August frowned, trying to think how he could persuade his mother to let him go.

"The National Gallery is just a few blocks away," said April. "Tell your mother you want to see the pictures."

"I'll try!" said August out loud.

The receptionist looked at him as if he were crazy, but he paid no attention. He went inside and asked his mother if he could go to the National Gallery to see the pictures.

"Alone? Certainly not!" said Mrs. Brown. "I'm stopping for lunch at one o'clock. I'll take you then."

She had been talking with another lawyer from the office. The lawyer, an older man, had already made friends with August. He slapped him on the back and said to August's mother, "Come on, give the kid a break! The National Gallery is just around the corner. Nothing can happen to him."

"That's what I've told myself every morning for a week," Mrs. Brown said gloomily, "and every day he gets into trouble of one sort or another." But she let him go.

The O'Malleys and Jeremiah Jenkins were waiting impatiently on the sidewalk. Bessie and Tessie swung their skates carelessly by the straps, but Jeremiah clutched his lovingly to his chest, as if they were a couple of kittens.

"Can't I put them on now?" he begged. "You could pull me!"

But April refused. "We'll give you a lesson when we're inside the museum. It's not as easy as you think."

The children went into the National Gallery by the entrance on Constitution Avenue. They tramped past the guards and up the curving marble staircase into the rotunda. While the twins and Jeremiah were fastening their skates, August stared around him in awe. He was standing in an enormous round space under a high dome. At the center of the space was a large fountain with a statue of Mercury rising out of the splashing water. Around the edge of the dome were twenty-four huge black marble columns. The floor was glossy black and white marble, laid down in circular patterns around the fountain. Two long galleries, lined with statues, led off from the rotunda. August agreed that it was an ideal place to skate.

Bessie and Tessie had often boasted about their skating style. Now August saw that they had good reason to boast. Arm in arm, they circled the fountain, twisted in and out of the marble columns, glided up and down the galleries. They twirled in dizzy circles, skated backward, threw their legs out in fancy pirouettes.

Meanwhile, poor Jeremiah had fallen nine times on his behind and twice on his nose. April and August propped him up by the elbows and walked him slowly back and forth, but Jeremiah fell again, dragging August down with him, and one of the guards gave August a suspicious look.

"You'd better just watch," said April. "And remember, don't talk—they'll think you're crazy."

The twins took time off to give Jeremiah a lesson, and soon he was moving along by himself—clumsily, but safely. Then the twins lent their skates to Mike and April, and Jeremiah grumblingly agreed to give Jessie a turn.

Mike and April were far from champion skaters, but they made up for it in fun. August was shocked to hear April, who was usually so well-behaved, yodel as she raced Mike to the end of a gallery and scream with laughter when Mike snatched the cap off the head of a puzzled guard. She careened around the fountain, and when she hurtled into Mike, who was careening in the other direction, she just picked herself up and started off again.

The twins shook their heads disapprovingly. "She has no style," said Bessie. "She isn't even trying!"

"It took us over forty years to develop our style," Tessie told August gravely. "Skating is an art, you know."

Jessie had not picked up the art of skating from her older sisters, but she was doing a lot better than Jeremiah. Keeping her eyes on her feet, she worked her way around the fountain. Then she took off down one of the galleries, clutching at the statues for support when she lost her balance.

When she reached the far end, there was a shout of

protest. One of the guards had grabbed her arm and was scolding her angrily: "What do you think you're doing? It's against the rules to skate in here!"

Jessie had never been noticed by anyone but August. She turned pale and stared speechlessly at the guard.

"Where are your parents?" the guard asked. "Come on, speak up or I'll call the police!"

Mike and April took off their skates and ran over to help Jessie. They tried to pull her away from the guard, but he held her more firmly than ever.

"Let me go!" Jessie wailed. "You're hurting me!"

The guard led her toward the information desk. "I'll let you go when someone comes to claim you, young lady, and not one minute sooner."

The other children clustered in a frightened circle.

"What are we going to do?" asked Mike. "It never happened before!"

For once April was at a loss. "I don't know! One of us could go back and get Mrs. Pettylittle. Everybody can see her, and she could claim Jessie. But what if they arrest her too?"

"How come that guard can see Jessie?" August asked. "No one else can! I bet the other guards think he's crazy."

The children followed the guard to the information desk and began to feel very sorry for him. He was pointing at Jessie and talking excitedly to the woman behind the desk. Several other guards had come over to see what was going on, and they were staring at the first guard with horror on their faces.

August walked up to the angry guard and whispered, "Why don't you just let her go? Can't you see they don't believe you?"

This only made things worse. The guard grabbed August by the collar and shook him. "This kid's in on it too!" he shouted. "It's against the law to roller-skate in a public museum!"

The woman at the desk smiled at August. "Can you tell me what's going on? I didn't notice anybody roller-skating."

"I don't know what he's talking about," August lied. "Please, could you tell him to let go?"

The guard let go of August's collar but kept a firm grip on Jessie's arm. He repeated his story over and over, but no one would take him seriously.

"You've been working too hard," the woman told him. "Maybe you ought to go home and rest!"

August pulled the other children away from the desk. "I'm going to get my mother," he told them. "She'll know what to do. You stay with Jessie, and I'll be back as soon as I can."

Mrs. Brown did not want to leave her work, but August looked so worried that she agreed to come.

"Roller-skating in a museum?" she said as they hurried back to the National Gallery. "They must be out of their minds!"

"Most people can't see them," August explained, "so they never got caught before. You have to help them!"

"Well, I'll see what I can do," said Mrs. Brown.

She found it hard not to laugh when she saw the scene

at the information desk. A large crowd had collected around the guard who was blushing and had tears in his eyes but would not change his story.

"Can't *anyone* see her?" he pleaded. "Am I going crazy?"

"I can't see her," Mrs. Brown whispered. "Can you?"

"Of course I can!" said August. "And there are the others, over by the fountain."

Mrs. Brown turned to look at the fountain. All she saw was Meggie, who had taken off her shoes and socks, climbed in, and was splashing water at everybody who walked by.

Mrs. Brown laughed at the bewildered faces of Meggie's victims. "Can't anyone see *her* either?" she asked.

"Only you," said August. "She wouldn't get away with it otherwise."

"I'm beginning to think there's some truth to your story," said Mrs. Brown. "Well, wish me luck—here goes!"

She pushed her way through the crowd and confronted the guard, who was wiping his forehead with a big white handkerchief and looking more wretched than ever.

"I'm a lawyer," she informed him, "and my advice to you is to release that poor child and find out why your colleagues are playing this ridiculous practical joke on you."

The guard was so astonished that he let go of Jessie and waved his arms around his head. "She believes me!" he shouted. "She's a lawyer, and she believes me!"

August never knew what happened next because his mother grabbed him by the elbow and hurried him out of the museum.

"Did Jessie get away?" she asked when they were on the street.

"Yes, thanks to you!" August threw his arms around his mother. Then he pointed down the street. "Look! There they are now!"

Mrs. Brown saw only Meggie, looking very small and very much alone. "Are you sure that child will get home safely?" she asked.

"Of course I'm sure!" said August. "She's been taking the streetcar for forty-three years."

His mother sighed. "Well, all I can say is, I hope none of my friends were in that crowd. Because if anyone saw me, I'll never live it down!"

**11**

August was awakened the next morning by the sun streaming through his window. It bounced from wall to wall, lighting up his toys, his books, even the clothes he had left in a heap on the floor. A cluster of sparrows bickered on the maple branch that he could see from his bed, and from down the street he heard the long, sweet song of a mockingbird. August ran to the window and looked out. After three days of rain, Georgetown had burst into flower. And it was only six-thirty; he had the whole day before him.

Even Michele felt better. When August came downstairs, she was sitting in the kitchen with a scarf around her neck, sipping tea. Her nose was red, and her hair looked as if she hadn't combed it for a week, but she grinned at him cheerfully.

"I think I'll live!" she announced as he walked into the kitchen.

August's mother was in a good mood too, and to celebrate it she was cooking bacon. When August smelled it, he felt hungry for the first time in days. He fished a piece out of the pan and nibbled it, burning his tongue. Ordinarily it annoyed his mother when he picked at the food she was cooking, but this morning she just laughed.

"What are your plans for today?" she asked, transferring half a dozen strips of bacon to August's plate.

August wondered how she could ask; there was only one place where he wanted to be when he was not at home! "Oh, I thought I'd go up to—" he began.

"Pineapple Place!" his mother and Michele interrupted in unison. They both laughed, but it was friendly laughter.

When his mother had left for work, August made himself a sandwich in case Mr. Sweeny was feeling poorly again. He had always been particular about what he put in his sandwiches, but this morning it did not take him long to decide. He put three strips of bacon on a slice of raisin bread, added a spoonful of egg salad, poured a dribble of maple syrup over the egg salad, and slapped a slice of rye bread on top.

Michele watched with interest. "Well—enjoy!" she said. She blew her nose, wound the scarf more snugly around her neck, and shuffled into the living room to watch television.

August was surprised to see no children playing outside in Pineapple Place. He knocked at April's door, and Mrs. Anderson let him in. August liked Mrs. Anderson better than any grownup woman he knew, not counting his mother. She was a little like his mother, in fact. She wore her brown hair tied back the same way and had the same friendly brown eyes that crinkled when she smiled. This morning she was wearing an apron. There was a smudge on her nose, and her hands were white with flour all the way up to the elbows.

"April is in the kitchen," she said as she wiped some flour off the doorknob with a corner of her apron. "She's helping me to bake some apple pies."

April wore an apron too, and she had looped her ponytails over the top of her head to keep them out of the way, but her hair was flecked with flour all the same, and there was an apple peel on her shoe.

"Guess what!" she cried when she saw August. "Tomorrow we're having a party, and you're invited!"

"It's a street party," Mrs. Anderson explained. "If it's good weather, we'll set up tables outside. Mr. Todd will play records, and each family has to prepare some food."

April was arranging apple slices in the pie shells. Every so often she popped a slice into her mouth. "That's why we all have chores this morning," she said, "but we can do what we like this afternoon."

"What's the party for?" August asked.

"It's a double birthday party," said April, giggling. "Mike is going to be fifty-three, and Mrs. Sweeny is going to be a hundred and nineteen!"

Mrs. Anderson frowned reprovingly at her. "That was in poor taste, April. Mrs. Sweeny is as young as she ever was, and likely to stay that way."

She explained to August: "We like to celebrate birthdays in Pineapple Place because we all love parties. But naturally we don't count the years. For one thing, it would cost us a fortune in candles!"

Mrs. Anderson put three pies into the oven and set three more aside to cook later. She gave April and August a large bowl of peas to shell, and set to work tidying the kitchen. Soon a hot, sugary smell filled the house, and Mr. Anderson burst into the kitchen.

"Apple pie!" he cried. "Is there a piece for me?"

"You can have a whole pie," said April, "but you can't have it until tomorrow. They're for the party."

August had not met April's father before. As he stood up and shook hands, he decided that he liked him very much indeed. His face was long and lean, and although it was wrinkled like a grownup's face, August thought he still looked like a boy. He wore a crisp white doctor's tunic and pants, but his shoes were old and scuffed, and one of the laces had come untied. He had April's hazel eyes, but whereas April's eyes twinkled only when she forgot to be serious, her father's twinkled all the time.

Mrs. Anderson gave her husband two slices of bread with jam to make up for the apple pie. When he had finished eating, he winked at April and went back to his work.

"But what does he do?" August asked. "No one is sick now. Why does he dress that way?"

"When no one is sick, he does experiments," April explained. "He's trying to find a cure for common colds, but so far it isn't going too well. And besides"— she leaned forward and whispered into August's ear—"my mother doesn't approve, but when he gets bored with common colds, he does crossword puzzles."

August's face grew sulky. "You're lucky! Both your parents are at home all day. My mom doesn't want to live with my dad, and she doesn't even like to live with me. She'd rather work in a stuffy old office all day long. When we lived in Vermont, she used to bake pies and things, like your mom."

Mrs. Anderson had heard about August's family from April. She was silent while she dried the last of the dishes. Then she sat down next to August and looked at him with a little frown on her face.

"I think you're mixing several problems together," she told him. "I'm sure your mother doesn't enjoy stuffy offices any more than you do, but she may be forced to work, and she may even enjoy her job. Did you ever think of that?"

August was so surprised to hear her taking his mother's side that he couldn't answer.

"And when it comes to apple pies," Mrs. Anderson continued, "I don't know how your mother feels about them, but I've been baking apple pies for half a century. I don't seem to age, so I may be baking apple pies forever—and that's no life for a woman!"

April was shocked. "Mother!" she gasped.

Mrs. Anderson stood up and sighed. "Don't think I'm not happy living in Pineapple Place with April and her father," she told August. "When I think how old we'd be if Mr. Sweeny hadn't moved us—why, April might be a married woman with children of her own!—

well, then I'm thankful. But back in 1939, before we moved, I was tired of sewing frills on curtains and giving canasta parties. I wanted to go back to college and work for a degree, but then it was too late."

Mrs. Anderson's words kept echoing in August's mind that morning. Every time he looked at her face, he saw his mother's face, as if the two women were standing there together. It was a relief when chores were over and they could join the other children in the street.

"What are we going to do today?" Mike O'Malley asked April.

August had plans of his own and couldn't wait to tell them. "I have an idea!" he said. "Have you ever been on the Metro?"

Mike shook his head. "We don't dare. It's the same old story: if we get trapped in a crowded place, people can feel us."

"But the Metro isn't crowded unless it's rush hour," said August. "It's even safer than walking down the street. Come on, you'll love it!"

The Metro did not go into Georgetown, so the children walked to the Dupont Circle station, about fifteen blocks away. August enjoyed the walk across Georgetown. The streets were lined with beautiful old houses and the sidewalks were paved with bricks. When they reached the top of the rise, they could see all the way to the other side of Rock Creek Parkway, where the high modern buildings were silhouetted against the sky and where downtown Washington, D.C., began. August was beginning to think that Georgetown was as nice a place to live as Vermont, and he hated to leave it for what he called the real city, but he wanted to show his friends from Pineapple Place something almost as exciting as a streetcar ride.

At first the Metro station looked dull. It seemed to be nothing but a cluster of low cement walls. But when the children came around the corner of one of the walls and saw the entrance, they were amazed: right out under the open sky and slanting steeply downward into a huge well in the ground was the longest escalator they had ever seen.

At first Meggie and Jeremiah were frightened to go on the escalator, but when they saw April, August, Jessica, and Mike start down ahead, shouting with excitement, they changed their minds and stepped on cautiously, each holding the hand of a twin.

What August liked about the escalator was that although he started out knowing that he was standing straight up and the well was slanted, after a while he began to think that the well went straight down and he was leaning forward. By the time he reached the bottom, he felt dizzy, and when he looked at the top of the well and saw the faraway, bright circle of sky, he felt even dizzier.

The children from Pineapple Place thought the escalator was such fun that they rode up and down four times, but they were not impressed by the Metro. Although they liked the machines that tell you how to buy your ticket and the machines that suck in your ticket at one end and spit it out at the other as you go through the gates, once they were on the platform, they were disappointed.

"There's artwork in the Paris metro," said April, "and people playing music. This metro is empty, and it's too quiet."

"It's not quiet during rush hour," August replied indignantly, "but you said you didn't want to go in a crowd!"

A train pulled almost noiselessly into the station, and the children filed in and sat down. After a moment's wait, the doors slid shut, and the train moved into a dark tunnel. The ride was so smooth that the only way to tell the train was moving was to watch the lights that flashed by out of the darkness.

The children were alone in the car, so August could talk freely. "Don't you think it's fun?" he asked.

"I can see how it would be," April conceded, "for someone from Vermont."

"The Paris metro was full of interesting smells," said Meggie. "This one just smells of plastic."

"And it's not bumpy enough," Mike added. "After all these years you'd think scientists could invent better bumps."

Just as August opened his mouth to argue, the train pulled into a station and several persons came into the car. At once August learned the dangers of being invisible: a fat old woman walked over and sat on Jeremiah's lap. Jeremiah screamed, but the fat woman didn't hear him. In fact, she didn't feel him either. She just beamed at August and said, "These seats are so comfortable, I declare I feel as if I were floating on air!"

Jeremiah moaned and wriggled, but April ordered him to stop. "It's your own fault for not getting out of the way," she told him severely, "so keep still until she gets up. If she feels you, she'll yell for help, and then what will we do?"

"You're always picking on me!" Jeremiah whined in a muffled voice. "I'm going to tell my mummy on you!"

Luckily the fat woman got off at the next stop, which was the children's stop too. August led them out to the street, where they blinked in the sunlight and took deep breaths of fresh air, as if they had been trapped for hours in a dark and stuffy cave instead of riding for a few minutes on a well-lit and air-conditioned subway.

August felt insulted. "I *was* going to take you to the White House," he said, "but maybe that isn't good enough for you either."

To his surprise, the children thought it was a wonderful idea. Their faces brightened, and they followed him cheerfully toward Pennsylvania Avenue.

"It's too bad we already had lunch," said Mike. "The White House is a terrific place for a picnic."

"A picnic in the White House?" August repeated incredulously.

"Not *inside* the White House," April explained. "Out on the lawn. Come on, I'll show you."

When they reached the White House, she pointed through the railings. "Do you see that little pool up there, right in the middle of the lawn? That's where we go. It's nice and shady in the summer, and we can wade. Once the President walked right past us. Mike wanted to bump him, but I told him it was disrespectful."

August was still in a bad mood about the Metro, and he felt like arguing. "Nobody is allowed to picnic on the White House lawn!" he shouted. "And I bet you never saw the President either. You're just showing off!"

Except for the children from Pineapple Place, who were invisible, no one was anywhere near August, so it looked as if he were shouting into thin air. A policeman began to saunter toward him.

"Now see what you've done!" said April. "We'd better get out of here!"

She looked around quickly for the younger children and discovered that Meggie and Jessie were missing.

"Where can they be?" she wailed. "They were here just a minute ago!"

She started to call, and the others joined in except for August, who had his eye on the policeman. "Meggie, Jessie, where are you? Meggie! Jessie!"

"Here we are!" answered two high voices from inside the White House grounds.

August peered through the railings and gasped: the little girls had stripped down to their underpants and were splashing happily in the small round pool on the White House lawn. He had never been so shocked in his life. For once the children from Pineapple Place had gone too far! Grabbing the railings with both hands, August leaned forward and shouted angrily, "Jessie!

Meggie! You put your clothes on and come right back out here!"

There was an astonished grunt behind him. August looked around and saw the policeman, and in the policeman's outraged face he saw trouble. Leaving the children from Pineapple Place to solve their own problems, August turned and ran as fast as his legs would carry him.

**12**

August ran up Pennsylvania Avenue until the White House was far behind him. Then, casting a cautious eye around for policemen, he took the next bus back to Georgetown.

When he had time to catch his breath, he began to feel ashamed. What would Mike think of him, running away from a policeman and leaving a bunch of girls in trouble? For invisible children, they certainly got into a lot of trouble, especially when one of them turned out not to be invisible after all. If his mother could see Meggie and the guard at the museum could see Jessie, one of them might get noticed at the White House too. August wondered what would happen if the President looked out his window and saw two little girls running on the White House lawn in their underpants.

When August got home, his mother was already back from work and having tea in the living room with Mrs. Snyder-Smith. "Where have you been all day?" she asked, offering him some toast.

"Oh, around," said August. He thought it wiser not

to mention Pineapple Place to Mrs. Snyder-Smith, who had been the first to tell him it did not exist.

"I wanted to bring Peter to meet you," said Mrs. Snyder-Smith, "but he went to the movies with his father. It's ridiculous that you two have been moping around with nothing to do when together you could be having so much fun!"

"I wouldn't say that August has nothing to do," said Mrs. Brown. "On the contrary, he's into mischief of one sort or another every minute of the day."

"He was into a smelly sort of mischief the last time I saw him," said Mrs. Snyder-Smith. "He was up to his elbows in garbage and talking to himself a mile a minute!"

Mrs. Brown looked inquiringly at August. "When was that?"

"I guess that was Tuesday," said August. "I was helping April and Mike to rag-bag."

"Who?" asked Mrs. Snyder-Smith. "Don't tell me you've made friends with that dreadful bag lady!"

August wished he had not begun to answer questions, but he couldn't stop now. "She isn't dreadful—she's nice!" he said. "But I wasn't rag-bagging with her. I was with a friend of mine."

"You were all alone," Mrs. Snyder-Smith insisted. "I remember thinking how strange it looked. Who is this friend?"

"Her name is April Anderson," said August. "You wouldn't know her."

Mrs. Snyder-Smith cocked her head to one side and

smiled coyly. "I'll bet my bottom dollar she lives in that imaginary alley you found off P Street. You can't fool me!"

August turned bright red and didn't know what to say, but to his surprise his mother answered for him.

"Nonsense!" she said. "I don't know about the alley, but April Anderson is a well-brought-up little girl, and if she was looking in the garbage, she must have had a good reason."

When August was alone with his mother, he asked her how she knew that April was well brought up.

"Because in my profession you are assumed innocent until you are proved guilty," said Mrs. Brown.

August thought it was brave of his mother to defend a person she couldn't see. As a reward, he told her what he had done that day, starting with apple pies and ending at the White House. When she heard about the two little girls on the White House lawn, Mrs. Brown laughed until she had tears in her eyes.

"Are they all as cute as Meggie?" she asked.

"Jeremiah is kind of pretty to look at," August told her, "but you don't notice because he's so awful. I guess you'd say Mike is cute with all that red hair, but he'd be embarrassed if you told him. I like Mike better than any boy I've met since Zachary. What am I going to give him for his birthday?"

Mrs. Brown thought for a while. "Are you sure this is a birthday party?" she asked. "From what you've said, it sounds as if they might be moving soon. Maybe it's a going-away party."

Deep inside, August had been worrying about the same thing, and it made his chest ache to think about it. There had been too much moving that year! First he and his mother had moved away from his father, and now Zachary Judge was moving to Chicago. How could he stand it if the people in Pineapple Place moved too? He would miss every single one of them, even Jeremiah.

The more he thought about it, the more August wished he could give a present to everyone in Pineapple Place, not just to Mike O'Malley. After supper he settled into the window seat with his diary and made a list. First he wrote down the names of the people in Pineapple Place, which came to sixteen. Then he counted his money. Even with the money Zachary Judge had paid back to him, he had just five dollars and eleven cents. It was hardly enough to buy a present for one person, let alone sixteen. He would have to find things in his own home and hope that his friends would understand.

August thought about Mrs. Sweeny first, because it was her birthday too. He really didn't know anything about her except that she was a nurse, so he went to the medicine cabinet and found a box of Band-Aids. They would come in handy for patching roller-skaters' knees.

The younger children were easy. Meggie had admired the teddy bear that sat on August's bed, and August was really too old for it. Jessie loved to draw, so he would give her the coloring book he never used and the markers that were almost as good as new. And as for Jeremiah, if he didn't appreciate August's baseball cards, he could always trade them with Mike for something else. But what about the twins?

"Do you have any old jewelry?" August asked his mother. "Just junk, I mean, that you don't use any more."

Mrs. Brown laughed. "I hope I never wear junk, but I'll see what I can find." She went upstairs and came back with two charm bracelets. "Will these do?" she asked. "They look a little shabby, but they'll brighten up if you put them in soapy water."

"They're perfect!" August cried. "The twins will love them!"

Next he turned his mind to the grownups in Pineapple Place. He wrote down several ideas and then crossed them out because they were things his mother would not want him to give away, but at last he came up with a satisfying list of gifts.

Because Mr. Sweeny, in spite of motion discomfort, liked to travel, August decided to give him his compass. His father had bought it for him the last time they went camping, and August almost changed his mind about giving it away until he remembered that Mr. Sweeny had allowed him to go back to *then* and ride the street-car.

The obvious present for Mrs. Pettylittle was a new supply of shopping bags, and Mrs. O'Malley could have the thimble out of his mother's sewing box. His mother never used a thimble, so she gave it to him gladly. There was an extra wrench down in the basement that Mr. O'Malley would find useful for repairs. Mrs. Jenkins could teach the younger children out of the math book that August brought with him from Vermont: she could erase the answers that he had penciled in.

August had no trouble thinking of presents for April's parents. He would give Mrs. Anderson his collection of odd mittens so that next winter she would have to knit only one of each pair; most of them looked easy to match. And as for Mr. Anderson, August planned to slip him some crossword puzzles when his wife was not looking. There was one in each of the newspapers in a big pile in the basement, and although it would take a long time to cut them all out, he didn't grudge the time for April's father.

August knew just what would make Mr. Todd happy. Going from room to room, he collected all the pencils in the house and sharpened them to stubs.

That left Mike and April, who were August's special friends. August knew what they would like, but he wasn't sure he could bear to part with the things he had in mind. If he gave them to Mike and April and they moved away, he would never see the things again. But on the other hand, if Mike and April moved, August wanted them to have something to remember him by forever. It took him a long time to decide, but when he set off for Pineapple Place the next day with a shopping bag full of presents, there were two packages at the very bottom that he had wrapped more lovingly than any of the others.

It was a warm, sunny Saturday morning, and the air smelled of flowers. The mockingbird was singing again in the top branches of a magnolia tree, and it made August feel like singing too. He hummed softly as he walked along until, turning the corner of P Street, his humming was drowned out by a louder noise. It was a wild mixture of laughing and shouting, shrill music, and an occasional firecracker, and it came from Pineapple Place.

When the people in Pineapple Place gave a party, there was no stinting in the trouble they took. Gaily colored streamers crisscrossed from window to window of the six houses. There were balloons attached to all the trees like clusters of exotic flowers. The O'Malleys had tied an American flag to a mop stick and hung it out a second-story window. Tables had been placed end to end and covered with starched white cloths, and crowded on the tables was more food than August thought six families could eat in a year.

Mr. Todd had brought his record player outside and put on a stack of seventy-eights that slapped down on the turntable, one after the other, blaring out fox trots and polkas and waltzes. When August joined the party, Mike O'Malley was dancing the polka with Mrs. Pettylittle, Mrs. Sweeny was dancing with Mr. Todd, and Mr. Sweeny was sitting in an armchair in the sun with a rug tucked around his knees.

"Happy birthday, Mike!" August shouted over the din. "Happy birthday, Mrs. Sweeny! Many happy returns!"

He hardly had time to put down his bag of presents before April, her cheeks flushed and her eyes twinkling more than ever, grabbed his hands and was galloping down the street. August did not know how to polka, but he could gallop as well as any other child. When April was out of breath, he took a turn with Bessie O'Malley, and then he went once up and down the street with Jeremiah's mother before the music stopped.

"Some party!" he gasped as he collapsed on the steps of April's house. "I'm surprised you haven't had any complaints from the neighbors."

"We never do," said April confidently. "Sometimes someone can see one of us, but you're the only person who ever found the street. And counting birthdays and all the holidays, we've had twenty-two parties a year for forty-three years!"

August was good enough at math to know that came to nine hundred and forty-six parties. If they were all like this one, it sounded like a good life.

"When do you have time to go to school?" he asked April.

"We've been going to school for forty-three years," she reminded him, "not counting before we moved, and we may be going to school forever, so there's no hurry. Besides, Mrs. Jenkins doesn't like it any better than we do."

When August thought of staying in fourth grade for forty-three years, not to speak of forever, he wondered if he didn't prefer his own life after all, but before he had time to think it over, someone tapped a spoon against a glass, the music stopped, and Mr. and Mrs. O'Malley stepped up on a homemade podium.

"Hush!" said April. "Mike's father is going to give the birthday speech!"

Standing arm in arm on the podium, Mike O'Malley's parents made the funniest pair of grownups August had ever seen. In the first place, they were as alike as brother and sister. Both were pudgy, red-headed, sloppily dressed in flashy party clothes, and grinning from ear to ear. Both were jiggling up and down in their shiny party shoes as if they might rise up and float away like a couple of balloons. Mrs. O'Malley held a crumpled sheet of paper, which she handed to her husband when he had finished bowing and beaming at his neighbors.

April made a face. "He makes the same speech each time," she told August scornfully. "You'd think after all these years he'd take the trouble to learn it by heart. After all, they have more birthdays than any other family on the street."

Mr. O'Malley began his speech by saying, "Unaccustomed as I am to public speaking. . . ."

What came next August never knew because he was too busy calculating how many times Mr. O'Malley had made that speech if he always used the same one. There were five O'Malley children and two parents; with seven birthdays a year for forty-three years, he must have made it three hundred and one times. How could he be unaccustomed to public speaking?

By the time August came to this conclusion, Mr. O'Malley had put away his paper and was formally wishing his only son a ripe old age, which August thought was downright silly considering that no one in Pineapple Place ever grew older.

When the O'Malleys stepped down from the podium, August hoped the dancing would begin again, but April told him that according to tradition, Mr. Sweeny would now give a speech of his own.

Frowning and mumbling, the old man threw the rug off his knees and,with the help of a silver-handled cane, climbed up on the podium. He cleared his throat three times, took a large white handkerchief from his pocket, blew his nose, and spoke the following words:

"Travel broadens the mind, and wisdom is better than rubies, but in much wisdom is much grief. Grief is itself a medicine. A faithful friend is the medicine of life, which makes grief a friend. But remember that the best of friends must part. Every parting gives a foretaste of death, but death is the greatest journey, and travel broadens the mind."

August listened carefully to every word of this speech, but found it confusing. In fact, he didn't realize the speech was over until Mr. Sweeny blew his nose a second time and the people in Pineapple Place broke into enthusiastic cheers.

"Is Mr. Sweeny going to die?" August asked April.

"Of course not!" she said. "No one in Pineapple Place ever dies, but we do travel a lot. I can't say it affects our minds, but Mr. Sweeny ought to know. He reads a lot of books and knows practically everything."

Now that the speeches were over, the party started up more merrily than ever. Mrs. Sweeny sang "Oh, Danny

Boy," in a quavering soprano voice, while Mr. Sweeny dozed off in his chair. Mr. and Mrs. O'Malley danced the Charleston on the podium, and Jeremiah, after much prodding from his mother, recited "The Charge of the Light Brigade," during which the other children slipped away and stuffed themselves with apple pie. Then Mike and August made a bet who could stand on his head on the podium for the longest time, and Mike insisted he would have won if all that upside-down pie hadn't made him feel so sick. To settle his stomach, he set off firecrackers until Mr. Sweeny woke up and ordered him to stop.

It was late in the day, when all the street was in shadow and the air was growing cool, when the food was gone down to the last crumb and even the grown-ups were tired of dancing, that August remembered his shopping bag.

"Don't you give presents on birthdays?" he asked April.

"Not any more," she said. "We never seem to find the right things at the right time. It isn't as if we could go out and buy them."

"Well, I didn't buy these things," said August, showing his packages, "but I have something for everybody, not just Mike and Mrs. Sweeny."

August had hoped that the people in Pineapple Place would like his presents, but he never imagined that his selections would be so wildly successful. Everyone was delighted, even Mr. Sweeny, who gazed at August's compass with a dreamy look on his face.

"It's an idea," he mumbled. "I wonder why I never thought of it before?"

August looked over his shoulder. "We're facing west-north-west," he announced.

"I think you've solved a problem for me, young man," said Mr. Sweeny. "What is the first major city we would reach if we traveled W-N-W as the crow flies?"

August shut his eyes and tried to picture the map of the United States. "I'm not positive," he said, "but I'd say Chicago."

Mr. Sweeny slipped the compass into his waistcoat pocket, closed his eyes, and sighed. "Chicago!" he whispered to himself. "The windy city—why not?"

Soon there were only two presents left at the bottom of the shopping bag. August reached in and pulled them out, smiling shyly as he handed them to Mike and April.

"These are for you," he said, "if you want them."

Inside Mike O'Malley's package was August's catcher's mitt, and inside April's was a pair of roller skates. Both children were speechless.

"I know they're not new," said August, misinterpreting their shocked faces, "but I couldn't afford anything new. And actually, a mitt is better when it's been broken in a little. This one has been broken in a lot!"

Mike O'Malley's eyes glowed, and at last he found his voice. "I never thought I'd find one, not in a thousand years!" he whispered. "And now I've got one of my own!"

"But what will you do without it?" April asked August. "And your skates—now you don't have any for yourself!"

"I can borrow yours if you're here," said August gruffly, "and if you're not here, I wouldn't want to skate anyway."

April walked August back to his own house. She held his hand all the way, but didn't say a word until they arrived at August's front door. There she dropped his hand and looked at him with tears in her eyes.

"You're the nicest person I've met in my whole life," she said, "and I've been alive for a long, long time!"

Then she turned and ran.

The first thought that came into August's mind the next morning was that he had eaten too much apple pie. He tried to remember how often he had gone back for a slice and figured that it added up to about a pie and a half. Rolling over and burying his head in the pillow, he swore that he would never eat apple pie again. To make things worse, a sickeningly sweet smell drifted up from the kitchen; it was Sunday, and his mother was making waffles. How was he going to get out of eating waffles? August decided to stay in bed until the smell went away.

The street outside was quiet; not many cars went past on Sunday. But there were other sounds if you took the trouble to listen. To keep his mind off his stomach, August counted the sounds. He could hear the faraway drone of an airplane. The neighbors were playing the radio so softly that he could hear only the deepest notes. Then there was the mingled chattering of birds in the trees and small children up the street.

There were also indoor noises: water running somewhere, and an occasional banging of pipes. Downstairs in the kitchen his mother was talking with Michele. Suddenly August sat bolt upright. That wasn't Michele's voice—there was only one voice it could be, but how was it possible? He jumped out of bed, threw on his clothes, and rushed downstairs.

April was sitting at the kitchen table with a plate of waffles set before her. Her eyes twinkled as she swallowed, wiped her mouth with a napkin, and said gravely, "Your T-shirt is on back to front!"

August looked from April to his mother and back to April again. He could hardly believe his eyes. "You're supposed to be invisible!" he said. "What happened?"

"All I know is I heard a knock at the door and there she was," said Mrs. Brown. "She didn't have to introduce herself because she's just the way you described her. So I thought it was about time we returned her hospitality."

April poured more syrup on her waffles and explained: "Mr. Sweeny made me visible, but only until three o'clock. Everybody can see me, not just your mother. I can't get over how strange it feels!"

"But why?" August demanded. "I don't understand!"

"He did it as a special favor," said April. "He's never done it for any of us before, but I told him I wanted to give you a present, and I can't do it unless I'm visible."

"What present?" August wanted to know.

But April refused to tell. She finished her breakfast and told August to hurry up with his own.

When August explained why he wasn't hungry, his

mother laughed and said that he could wait until lunch. "Would you and April like to come back and eat here?" she asked.

"A picnic would fit in better with my plans," April said mysteriously. "I'll help you if you like."

August couldn't believe he would ever be hungry again, but just in case he made himself a relish and honey sandwich on oatmeal bread.

When April saw it, she was horrified. "I never saw anything so disgusting in my life!" she cried. "I'd like ham and cheese, please, and you can make two of them."

August started buttering the bread. "Why two? Is one of them for Mike?"

"Don't ask questions," said April.

With April's help, August packed a picnic big enough for three hungry children. Then April thanked Mrs. Brown politely for breakfast, and they went outside.

"Let's go to the Hyde School playground," April said. "I want to try out my new skates."

"But you said we were in a hurry!" August protested. "You can go skating any old day, but this is the first time I ever got to see you without the others!"

"Skating is part of my plan," said April firmly. "Just do what I tell you and don't ask questions."

The playground was deserted except for a boy who was standing still and slapping a ball half-heartedly into a catcher's mitt. At first August thought it was Mike O'Malley, but when he got closer, he saw that it was only Peter Snyder-Smith.

April waved at the boy, but he didn't wave back. Then she fastened her new skates and moved forward, cautiously at first, then faster. Halfway across the playground she twirled around and began skating backward. Peter Snyder-Smith looked up with interest on his face.

"I bet you can't do this!" April shouted at him.

Still skating backward, she worked up more and more speed until, wobbling dangerously on one leg, she leaned forward and kicked the other leg up behind her in a clumsy arabesque. Unfortunately this lasted for only one second because she hit a bump and fell down with a crash. August couldn't understand: it almost looked as if she had done it on purpose.

"You idiot!" he shouted as he ran to pick her up.

Peter Snyder-Smith was running too, and together they helped April off the ground. One of her knees was bleeding, but she tossed her head bravely and said, "I'm all right. It doesn't hurt."

"You ought to clean it," said Peter. "Wait a minute. I'll be right back."

He ran to the water fountain and wet a corner of his shirt. "It'll sting for a minute," he told April when he came back, "but I read somewhere that if you leave dirt in a wound, you can get gangrene."

April bit her lip while he cleaned her knee. "Thanks," she said, "it's okay now." She took a dirty handkerchief out of her pocket and tied it around her knee. A patch of red seeped through.

August was horrified. "Don't you think you'd better

go back and have Mrs. Sweeny put something on it?" he asked.

"Of course not!" said April. "I guess I won't skate any more today, though. I tell you what—let's go down to the canal. I know a perfect place for a picnic."

She took off her skates and tested her bad knee. "It's not bleeding any more, and it still bends," she told Peter Snyder-Smith. "Let's go! Can you come too? We have enough lunch for three."

Peter looked suspiciously at August and was about to refuse, but then he looked at April again and accepted.

The C and O Canal is no longer used for barges, but part of it has been made a national park. You can ice-skate on it in winter or fish in it in summer, and its long, flat towpath is perfect for running or bicycling. August, April, and Peter walked along slowly, keeping an eye out for water animals and baby ducks. August and Peter tossed the baseball back and forth, and before long they were in the middle of a discussion. It turned out that Peter was in fourth grade at Hyde School, and after August had asked him a few questions, he began to think it wouldn't be so bad after all. The teacher sounded nice, and Peter had a lot of friends.

"Where do *you* go to school?" Peter asked April.

"It's a very small private school," she told him. "You wouldn't know it."

"I bet I would," Peter insisted. "What's it called?"

April took so long to reply that August answered for her: "It's called the—um—Jeremiah Jenkins Academy."

"That must be new," said Peter. "I never heard of it."

"It's not exactly new," said August. "It's just that it's small. There are only about two kids in each class."

Peter looked puzzled, but before he could ask any more questions, they arrived at April's picnic spot. Half a mile out of Georgetown the towpath crosses a wooden bridge. Here some of the water slips over the side of the canal and goes cascading down a steep, rocky slope to meet the Potomac River below. A short way through the trees there is a wall that projects over the cascade. The three children walked out to the end of this wall and sat down in a row for their picnic.

Besides the sandwiches, there were apples and carrot sticks, potato chips and cheese. Both April and Peter were ravenous, but August was still feeling the effects of apple pie. He ate one carrot stick and half of his honey and relish sandwich. The other half he gave to Peter, who admitted that it tasted better than it looked. The children saved their crusts to feed to the ducks, and after finishing their meal, they set off to find some ducks.

August loved the canal because it was a strip of country that led into the city. He knew that raccoons lived in the banks and prowled the streets of Georgetown at night to raid the garbage pails. There were also water rats, snakes, and frogs. He could have spent hours hunting for the fluffy little wild ducklings that hid among the reeds, and he was glad to see that Peter enjoyed it too. But April seemed nervous and kept looking at her watch—an old-fashioned pocket watch repaired by Mr. Todd, which she carried in her skirt pocket.

"Let's start back!" she kept begging. "It's getting late, and I promised I'd be home by three."

The boys turned reluctantly toward Georgetown, dragging their feet and stopping now and then to toss a pebble into the canal.

"Do you have a mitt?" Peter asked.

August shook his head. "I used to, but I gave it away."

April was several yards ahead, trying to encourage them to hurry up. She heard Peter's question and called back: "If you really want to know, he gave it to a friend of mine who couldn't afford one of his own."

Peter was impressed. "I'll share mine if you like, until you get another."

He pulled the mitt off and let August have a turn. The two boys tossed the ball back and forth, laughing when one of them had to dash down the banks of the canal to retrieve it. They forgot to hurry in spite of April's pleas.

Far up the hill the university bell tolled three before Peter looked around and asked, "Where's your friend?"

April had disappeared. The footbridge that crossed the canal and led to 34th Street was already in sight, but August was sure she hadn't had the time to reach it. He peered down the wooded slope that led to the river, but she was nowhere to be seen.

"She said she had to be home by three," Peter reminded him. "She probably took off when we weren't looking."

August knew that April would no longer be visible to Peter when the clock struck three, but why couldn't he see her himself? Had she really had enough time to run away, or was she invisible to August now too?

"I'd better find out what happened," he told Peter as they walked up the hill toward home. "Thanks for lending me your mitt—I'll see you in school tomorrow!"

August went to his house first to see if April had gone back to visit his mother, but she wasn't there.

"It's after three," Mrs. Brown reminded him, "so I wouldn't see her anyway."

"I'll just run up to Pineapple Place and make sure she's all right," said August. "She hurt her knee when she was skating—maybe that's why she went home."

But his mother objected. "Do you realize that I've barely had a glimpse of you for the past ten days?" she asked. "I'm delighted that you found some friends, but couldn't we spend some time together for once?"

August remembered the hours he had spent exploring Washington with his mother when they first moved in, and he wondered whether she had begun to feel lonely after he met the people in Pineapple Place.

"I'm sorry!" he said. "I didn't mean to leave you all by yourself."

"Nonsense!" said Mrs. Brown. "I've been making friends of my own. In fact, one of them is right up the street. I think I'll be seeing a lot of Mrs. Snyder-Smith, even though you've taken a dislike to her son."

"Who, me?" cried August. "Why should I dislike Peter? He's terrific!"

Mrs. Brown was surprised, but she asked no questions. "Let's walk up to the Dumbarton Oaks Gardens," she suggested. "I'll buy you an ice-cream cone on the way."

As they walked through Georgetown licking their ice-cream cones, August pointed out his favorite spots. "There used to be a grocery store on that corner, right where the dress shop is," he said, "and that's where I found the skate, in a little street just a block down that way."

Mrs. Brown listened thoughtfully. After a while she asked, "So you really don't mind living here?"

"Mind!" cried August. "I love it! It's just about as good as home."

"But this *is* home now," his mother reminded him gently, "except when you go back to Vermont to visit your father."

"Well, I like both places just fine," said August, "so you don't have to worry. And that school is going to be okay too. Peter Snyder-Smith says so, and he ought to know."

Mrs. Brown was silent until they reached the Dumbarton Oaks Gardens. Then, as they walked up the gravel driveway, she smiled at August and said, "I *was* worried about you at first, you know. You looked so unhappy and you were . . . not rude, but sort of exclusive, if you know what I mean. As if you wouldn't forgive me for leaving your father and moving down here and getting a job."

August didn't like to talk about the divorce, but the job was a different matter. "Why shouldn't you have a job?" he asked. "It's no life for a woman to sit at home all day sewing frills on curtains and giving canasta parties."

Mrs. Brown stared at her son in amazement. "Frills?" she repeated. "Canasta parties? What on earth are you talking about?"

August didn't answer because another question came into his mind. "April said Mr. Sweeny made her visible so that she could give me a present," he told his mother. "What do you suppose it was?"

**14**

The first day at school went by like a breeze. Now that the building was full of children, August couldn't remember why he had once found it grim. His new teacher put him next to Peter Snyder-Smith because he was the only pupil August knew, but before school was over, August knew the name of every child in class and had already picked out the children he wanted for his friends. He was relieved to discover that although the fourth-grade reader was harder than the one he used in Vermont, he was way ahead in math. He played basketball with Peter and some other boys at recess, and they traded desserts at lunch. For something he had been dreading for weeks, school was a big success.

August hurried home that afternoon. He wanted to leave his books and get a bite to eat before he went up to Pineapple Place to tell April about his first day at school. Michele was on the phone when he walked into the kitchen. She stopped talking for a moment and put her hand over the receiver.

"There's a package for you," she said, "out on the living room table."

The package had obviously not come in the mail; it had no stamps and no address. There was no return address on it either: only AUGUST BROWN in large capital letters. August pulled off the string and ripped apart the paper. Inside was a turtleneck sweater knitted every color in the rainbow, and a letter from April Anderson:

Dear August,

I'm really sorry to leave without saying good-by, but I warned you it might happen. Don't worry, we'll see each other again. I asked Mr. Sweeny, and he said that once you've been to Pineapple Place, you belong forever. Meanwhile, I hope you like the friend I gave you.

Love,
April

"Oh, no!" August wailed. "Oh, my golly, no!"

Michele hung up the phone and came into the living room. "What's the matter? Bad news?"

"I don't know yet," August shouted as he ran out the front door. "I have to go see."

He tore down to the corner and crossed N Street with hardly a glance for traffic. He ran up 35th Street faster than he had ever run in his life. By the time he turned right on P Street, he had a stitch in his side. Someone shouted, "Hey, Speedy, where's the fire?" but August paid no attention. Panting and hugging his arms around his chest, he stared at the houses across the street. Number 3413 and number 3415 were standing shoulder to shoulder, the pink brick wall nestled up against the yellow brick wall without an inch of space between. Pineapple Place had moved away from Georgetown.

That night at supper August pushed the food around his plate and didn't eat a bite. His mother noticed, but she said nothing, even when Michele took the plate away and put it in the sink.

"How was your first day at school?" Michele asked.

"Fine," said August, "just fine."

"Like your new teacher?"

"She's fine too," said August. "Everything is fine."

His face was so glum that his mother stopped eating and looked concerned. "Something is wrong," she said. "You'd better tell me about it."

August scraped back his chair and stood up, turning away from his mother and Michele so that they wouldn't see the tears in his eyes. "They moved," he said.

"Everybody," Mrs. Brown asked, "or just April?"

"All six families," said August. "The whole street moved. I went and looked, after school, and it just isn't there any more. And what I want to know is, Why?"

His mother took a bowl of fruit salad out of the refrigerator. "Sometimes it's better not to question things," she said. "Are you having any dessert, August?"

"Can you keep it for later?" he asked. "I think I'll go do my homework."

In spite of fourth grade and Peter Snyder-Smith, August felt miserable for the next few days, but when he came home from school on Friday, he found a letter from Zachary Judge. It had been written on Sunday and was postmarked Chicago:

Dear Aug,

Our new house would be okay if it weren't in the city, but my new school stinks. I don't know anybody in my class, and there's nobody I want to know. I was thinking of hitchhiking back to Vermont, except I made friends with a boy in the park this afternoon who says he knows you. He has your catcher's mitt. If you didn't want your catcher's mitt, why didn't you let me keep it?

Your friend,
Zack

August threw his book bag on the window seat and read the letter over again three times. If Zachary met Mike O'Malley on Sunday afternoon, Mr. Sweeny must have moved Pineapple Place just after April disappeared from the towpath. No wonder April was in such a hurry to get home! So now they were in Chicago. Where would they be, August wondered, if he had not given Mr. Sweeny his compass?

August crumpled up Zachary's letter and stuffed it

into his pocket. He sat down in the window seat and stared out at the street. A man in bathing trunks jogged by on the opposite sidewalk. Mrs. Snyder-Smith was walking her dog, and Peter was outside his house down the block, dribbling his basketball. In a while August would join him; the days were growing longer, and there were hours left to play.

But August had something more important to do first. He ran to get his diary and sat down to start a new list. At the top of the page marked *April 23, 1982,* he wrote: "REASONS WHY I LIKED THE PEOPLE IN PINEAPPLE PLACE."

He numbered the lines from one to thirty and leaned back to think about it.